'Do you always kiss the hired help goodbye?' Catherine asked.

'Of course not!' He walked to the door and looked back at her tauntingly. 'Mrs Jarvis is a respectable widow and the cleaner is at least eighty. That just leaves you and, as I'm in an exuberant mood, you just chased after me at the right time.'

'I did not chase after you!' Catherine stormed, but all she got was a mocking grin.

'Then work it into your schedule,' he advised.

Dear Reader

This is the time of year when thoughts turn to sun, sand and the sea. This summer, Mills & Boon will bring you at least two of those elements in a duet of stories by popular authors Emma Darcy and Sandra Marton. Look out next month for our collection of two exciting, exotic and sensual desert romances, which bring Arab princes, lashings of sun and sand (and maybe even the odd oasis) right to your door!

The Editor

Patricia Wilson was born in Yorkshire and lived there until she married and had four children. She loves travelling and has lived in Singapore, Africa and Spain. She had always wanted to be a writer but a growing family and career as a teacher left her with little time to pursue her interest. With the encouragement of her family she gave up teaching in order to concentrate on writing and her other interests of music and painting.

Recent titles by the same author:

A DANGEROUS MAGIC
A HEALING FIRE
POWERFUL STRANGER

EDGE OF DANGER

BY

PATRICIA WILSON

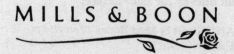

MILLS & BOON LIMITED
ETON HOUSE, 18-24 PARADISE ROAD
RICHMOND, SURREY TW9 1SR

*First published in Great Britain 1994
by Mills & Boon Limited*

© Patricia Wilson 1994

*Australian copyright 1994   Philippine copyright 1994
This edition 1994*

ISBN 0 263 78545 9

*Set in Times Roman 10 on 11¼ pt.
01-9407-56720 C*

Made and printed in Great Britain

CHAPTER ONE

'WE'RE finished, Catherine. The firm is as good as wiped off the face of the map, and there's nothing at all we can do about it.'

Catherine Farrell stood in the managing director's office and looked with shocked sympathy at her boss's despondent face.

'But how can it have happened? We're making money even in these hard times. Things are rolling along all right. With a few good orders we could have been on our feet again in no time at all. This is a sound business.'

'If it hadn't been sound, King wouldn't have been interested,' George Darriel grunted. 'The fact of the matter is that we're in a weak trough at the moment and Damon King has swooped. No shareholder could resist his offer. I've seen it coming, but it was a bit like watching a train approaching with no hope of stopping it.'

'He's a terrible man!' Catherine asserted angrily. 'He just tears firms apart.'

'And puts them back together again,' George Darriel finished wryly. 'As he thinks we're worth a take-over he'll pour money into the firm and have it back on its feet with great speed. He's just about the cleverest businessman in the country. When the King Group swoops there's just nothing to be done about it. He never makes a move until everything is sewn up tightly.'

'So what will you do?' Catherine asked compassionately.

Darriel Glassware was a very old firm, owned by the same family for nearly a hundred years. It was like wiping out past and future generations in one go. It might be good business, but to Catherine it was simply cold-blooded.

'Me? I'll take the money and have a good think,' George Darriel muttered. He looked up at her ruefully. 'What will you do is more to the point. All the office staff will have to go. He'll bring his own people in. Production will continue while he assesses everything, so I've got hopes for the men at the works. Everyone else goes, though. That was laid down very firmly, and I'm to deal with it. He'll move his own staff in next month.'

'I expect I'll cope,' Catherine said bravely. 'There are other jobs.'

'Not many, Catherine. It's damnable! You're the best assistant I've ever had. You know the firm inside out. At least he could have kept *you* on.'

'He doesn't sound particularly altruistic,' Catherine murmured. 'I expect we're all just bits of paper to be moved around as far as he's concerned. He won't even know who we are.'

George Darriel nodded glumly, and there was no point in dragging it out further. Damon King had struck at the firm like lightning, and they were all so much history.

She was quite used to hearing the name King, although she had never seen him, not even a picture in the Press. He had been a force in the business world since he was in his early twenties, a millionaire at thirty, and was utterly ruthless. He was a tycoon who had an almost uncanny way of making money.

In a way he permeated her own small family too, because her brother worked for the mighty King Group, even though it was in a lowly capacity, and now he had struck very close to home indeed, because she would soon be out of work. Putting a brave face on it was one thing; managing without her job was yet another.

She wondered how her brother would react to this news. If she couldn't get another job he was going to have to take a bit more responsibility than he had been taking recently. Robin was obsessed with an entirely different future, and he was a daily worry to her. He had not been like that before he went to work for the King Group. It seemed that everything Damon King touched turned sour—even people.

Three weeks later, Catherine watched Robin warily, waiting for the outburst that came at this time every morning, and she was not disappointed.

'I hate the damned job!' He snapped the words out as usual, his face set and annoyed.

'I know,' Catherine assured him patiently. 'You tell me every day.'

Apparently her tone irritated him further, because he actually glared at her.

'I must have been mad to take the job in the first place,' he muttered. 'It's not what I want to do, and you know it, Cath.'

'I know it now,' she agreed calmly. 'I also remember that at university you thought it was the best thing in the world to train to be an accountant. You were very proud and dedicated. It was all part of your big plan for life. I ought to remind you too that people don't *take* jobs with the King Group. They beg on their knees and get turned down. To go straight from your professional training to a job like that was almost miraculous. You're lucky, Robin, and they wouldn't have taken you if you weren't good.'

'I'm not lucky,' he insisted angrily. 'You know I only went there to further my real career.'

Catherine nodded and decided to keep quiet. Talking did no good. It was perfectly true that he had gone to university with high hopes of a career in accounting, but he had quickly discovered another talent, one that interested him a great deal more—and she couldn't blame him really. He was a very good musician. He had played the guitar and sung with a college group, and now he wanted to continue. His interest in anything else was completely gone.

Duty had kept his nose to the grindstone so far, made him finish his exams, but she had the uneasy feeling that it wouldn't last. He was really a square peg at the great offices in the heart of the city, and his plans had misfired.

To someone like Robin it might have seemed a good idea to get into the firm that Damon King owned. Crown Records was part of the King Group, and they never backed a loser. The black crown that was their trademark was famous, but it was merely a hobby for Damon King, a sideline. It probably didn't give him as much pleasure as his real work, though—smashing businesses.

'All I have to do is get Damon King to notice me,' her brother had said at the first. 'He's clever, and he knows talent when he sees it. I'll be famous in no time, right at the top.'

That had been a long time ago, but, in spite of hopeful days, the powerful boss of the King Group had never turned his head in Robin's direction.

To be fair, Catherine couldn't blame the mighty Mr King, although she was quite ready to blame him for just about anything. How could the great man be expected to know that one of his junior accountants was a genius with the guitar and a future pop star? She didn't suppose Damon King went round his offices like a talent scout. He was much too busy turning his eyes on inoffensive family firms.

'You'll miss the bus,' she murmured, and Robin grunted with further irritation.

'Day in, day out. On the bus, off the bus. Into the office and out again, looking like this!' He glanced down at his dark suit and glowered further.

'You look very smart,' Catherine placated. 'You can hardly go to those prestigious offices in jeans and a T-shirt. You *would* be noticed then!'

'Hey!' Robin's face took on a very cunning expression, his eyes gleaming, and Catherine shook her head firmly.

'Forget I spoke,' she ordered. 'You'd be fired on the spot and you still wouldn't be a pop star. This is my last week, unfortunately. It would leave both of us out of work; then what would happen?'

'I'm sorry, Cath.' Robin looked contrite, his once normal expression reasserting itself. 'You've worked really hard and you're good at your job. The perfect PA and now the firm is folding under you.'

'It's being *crushed* under me,' Catherine corrected crossly. 'I've been searching for another job ever since I knew about the take-over, but there's not a single bright cloud on the horizon.' She quickly cleared the breakfast dishes and looked at her watch. She would be late herself if she didn't hurry.

'Something will come up,' Robin stated brightly, and she grimaced.

'The dole queue?'

He grinned at her, aiming a kiss at her cheek and making for the door. Catherine waited for it to slam, wincing when it did. Robin left in the same flurry of noise each day, but at least he had left in a better frame of mind this time. She knew it wouldn't last long. This urge to perform had become almost like a disease.

'He's gone, I hear.' Her grandfather came slowly down the stairs and smiled at her. 'Did you get the morning lecture?'

'I did. Oh, Gramps! Why can't you stay in bed when you're told?' she remonstrated anxiously. 'You don't look too well. I was just about to bring your tray up.'

'Be off with you, girl,' he grunted. 'I'll not be molly-coddled. You'll miss your bus.'

'I don't suppose it would matter,' Catherine sighed, gathering her things. 'There's only this week.'

'We'll manage,' Gramps said cheerfully. 'Anyway, something's sure to turn up.'

Catherine nodded dutifully. Her grandfather had used almost the same words that her brother had spoken a few seconds earlier. He was very much like Robin at heart, ever hopeful. It was strange that she felt so responsible for both of them when she was the youngest person in the household.

As she went for her bus Catherine still worried about her grandfather. She and Robin had no other relatives. Gramps had taken them in when they were very young, and he was old now and ill. His heart was not strong, but it was the last thing he would have admitted, because he still liked to feel that he looked after them.

In fact Catherine felt the whole burden herself, because Robin could not be relied on now. He was merely putting on a false face at the office, his dreams eating into him. He really did have talent, but if he thought that Damon King would ever notice him in any other capacity than that of a lowly employee he was mistaken.

Robin came home with a very secret smile on his face that evening, and Catherine simply waited. Whatever it was, he would tell her, because he could never keep things to himself. He kept quiet until after dinner when Gramps went to get an early night, then he almost exploded with his news.

'Damon King wants a personal assistant!'

He sat back, smiling triumphantly, and Catherine looked at him in astonishment, wondering why the knowledge pleased him so much. It really was nothing to do with them.

'Which can be taken to mean—what?' she asked finally when he just sat there grinning.

'You can apply!' Robin leaned forward, his face filled with enthusiasm. 'Just think, Cath, PA to Damon King! You'd be really close to him and you could work his thoughts round to me. This is my lucky day!'

'Cancel your dreams.' Catherine sighed. 'I wouldn't even get an interview. I'm too young, and I've only worked in a small firm. The King Group is big business, right at the top of the tree. The city quakes when Damon King takes a deep breath. Crown Records is just a toy to him, even though you think of nothing else. He's *powerful*, important. I wouldn't even get to the door of that great big building, and if I did, they'd pick me up by my coat lapels and put me out like the cat.'

'You're beautiful!' Robin looked indignant, and Catherine gave him an amused glance.

'Thank you, but we're talking hard-headed businessman, dangerous predator. King is not a youth, choosing his staff for their looks. In any case, glamorous women fight to attract his attention, or so I've read. He's got a certain reputation, apparently.'

'You seem to know a lot about him,' Robin stated slyly, and this time she gave him the benefit of a heated glance.

'He's squeezed me right out of a job! My interest in him is of the malevolent variety. In any case, I've been reading about him for ages. I have no idea at all what he looks like. I wouldn't know him if I saw him, but I do know he should be avoided. I wish you didn't have to work there, and I'm certainly not throwing *myself* into the cauldron, just to get you launched into the glitter of showbusiness.'

'You'll never get such a chance again,' Robin muttered.

'I haven't got a chance now!' Catherine pointed out impatiently. 'I'm only just twenty-four, relatively inexperienced and too wary to put myself in the firing-line. In any case, he'll be looking for an older woman with a military bearing, probably someone with a thick skin who'll take his daily attacks on other firms with a shrug of the shoulder and a pleased smile.'

'I don't care how many firms he devours,' Robin retorted, his irritability growing. 'I'm just interested in that part of the King Group called Crown Records. If you knew him you could get me an audition.'

'Oh, stop it, Robin! Do you imagine he does it himself?' Catherine asked crossly. 'He just appears when the artist has been polished, wallows in the glory, collects the cash, and walks off. In any case, this is all pointless. As I've told you, I wouldn't stand a chance.'

'You could try,' Robin grumbled. 'The post hasn't been advertised yet. It's only going round by word of mouth. You could get your word in first.'

'What did he do with his last PA?' Catherine enquired ironically, and her brother shrugged, his expression tight.

'She's getting married.'

'Any port in a storm,' Catherine murmured, getting up to make coffee.

'It shows she's young.'

'It shows nothing of the sort. People of all ages marry. People of my age do not get PA jobs with somebody like Damon King, so drop the subject.'

'You were my last hope.' Robin looked tragic, very dramatic, trying out his acting ability, anything to get round her, and Catherine hid a smile. Some hope! She would be lucky to be the tea lady in a powerful firm like that.

All the same, it was another application form to fill in, even if they fell about laughing at the great big King Group. She couldn't hit out personally at Damon King for all the trouble he had caused her, but she could waste their time with a letter and maybe even an application form.

When a slack moment came next day at work she wrote for a form, totally forgetting that she had the information from an insider source. If they sent a form she would fill it in. She had nothing to lose. If they laughed she wouldn't even know it.

They sent a form, and her own boss took it in his stride, grinning at her and then allowing his name to be used for reference purposes.

'May as well go for gold, Catherine.' He laughed. 'They can't kill you for sheer cheek. At least it would give me a laugh if you got it. It would be like putting the cat in among the fat pigeons, and all done so quietly.'

Oddly enough, she hadn't looked at it like that—sheer cheek. It had been an almost defiant gesture. That firm, that man, had interfered with her life, and she resented it. Damon King had left her without a job after this week, and she had to take care of Gramps.

Robin had been utterly changed since he had worked there too and was getting more odd every day. Everything he did at work must be quite mechanical, because his mind was almost always on the latest gig, some new song, a club appearance. Robin's nights were much more important to him than his days, and she knew deep inside that taking care of Gramps would be down to her.

Not that sheer cheek mattered. If the form had been sent out by a clerk, it would certainly not be vetted by some underling, and her age and relative inexperience would be noticed. She sent it off, however, putting it into the post-box with an air of grim irritation. She wouldn't at all mind getting in with the fat pigeons. It was like tossing down the gauntlet—pity that nobody would pick it up!

After a week she had forgotten all about it, and Robin for once was silent on the subject of the King Group. Catherine was scanning the papers with more anxiety every day. There were no jobs in her bracket at all, and now that she had finished work there was a rather desperate feeling inside her. She couldn't afford to be out of work. Any day now Robin might be sacked; she felt it in her bones. Nobody could be busy day and night and perform properly.

Gramps looked on the bright side as usual, but Catherine spent her time worrying, not least about her grandfather's health and his future comfort. Each day he looked more frail, and now that she was home all the time he couldn't hide it from her quite so well.

She wanted to do things for him, protect him from the outside world, repay his years of loving care. If anything happened to Gramps she just didn't know what she would do, because she wasn't close to Robin any more. He had slowly changed.

When the letter came offering her an interview she couldn't believe it at all.

'I've actually got an interview!'

'Told you so!' Robin smirked at her. 'It's probably fate.'

'It's probably some horrendous mistake,' Catherine muttered, imagining herself standing there as they apologised—and laughed. 'It can't be true.'

'Don't be so defeatist,' Robin ordered. 'New blood is needed in any thriving firm from time to time. He probably wants to train you to his ways and keep you beside him forever.'

'He won't even have seen this yet,' Catherine surmised. 'By the time any forms get to him, the rejects will have been sorted—that's me.'

Robin had that gleam back in his eyes, and Catherine felt nervous. She felt as if she had inadvertently stepped into a very big hole and that it just might be bottomless. She didn't feel like an avenging cat now.

She spent the whole evening in her room, practising looking older, but it was all a failure. Her jet-black hair was thick and luxurious, down below her shoulders, although she wore it up for work. Even then, there was no mistaking the youth in her clear grey eyes. The fact that she was very slender was also a disadvantage. She felt she would have been taken more seriously if she had carried a bit more weight and a lot more age.

She sighed at her reflection in the mirror. Who was going to believe that she was good at her job? They would take one look at her and decide she was completely unsuitable. Still, looking on the bright side, it would save her from the ordeal of meeting Damon King.

She wanted a good job, but she didn't want to work with him. She really regretted sending off that form. All she had wanted to do was cause a bit of bother, and now it was coming back. The gauntlet she had imagined tossing down might very well turn out to be a boomerang.

It was like a police interrogation in a film, Catherine decided when she finally came face to face with the people interviewing her. Apparently it was not the done thing to let one applicant see another, and she was all alone until she was called into what appeared to be a boardroom. By then she was fairly demoralised.

It was going to be difficult talking about her past experience and future aspirations. Her experience was limited, her aspirations bordering on the simple—a wish to survive.

They didn't sit her under a glaring lamp and demand to know all, but the similarity was decidedly there. She sat at a table facing straight into the sunlight, and it must have been deliberate. It was also rather intimidating.

Three people were interviewing her, throwing questions at her with little pause in between, and somewhere on the sidelines there was another man simply looking. She had not had the chance to see him, because she was seated and the whole thing under way before she could even glance round.

Irritation kept her wits about her. The sunlight was streaming in through the window and it was hot in the room, even on a cool spring afternoon. She would have liked to take off her coat, but nobody invited her to do so, and after a while she decided that their manner was not to her liking at all. They were simply going through the motions now that they could see her.

Catherine's eyes flashed. It put her on her mettle. If she didn't stand a chance, then there was no point in edging around things diplomatically.

'You're very young.' One of the men made this statement with an air of definite disapproval, and Catherine squinted at him through the sunlight.

'At the moment,' she agreed. 'I expect to age, given time.'

'You seem to have crammed a lot into twenty-four years,' another one pointed out. He seemed to be laughing to himself, and Catherine didn't like that either.

'If you mean I've worked hard, then yes, I have,' she assured him briskly. 'I wanted to work my way up quickly——'

'But you decided to take a short cut and apply right for the top?' he cut in.

It became really obvious that they were not taking her seriously, any more seriously than she had imagined they would; in fact they were bordering on the antagonistic. Catherine threw caution to the winds.

'Only because nothing more interesting came up,' she rejoined tartly. If they had brought her here for intellectual amusement, then she could play that game too.

The next question quite threw her off balance, though, and her defiance collapsed.

'You wrote for an application form before the job was advertised, Miss Farrell,' one of them murmured. 'It intrigued us. You're gifted with second sight?'

'Er—I...' Catherine's face flushed, and she had no idea how to get out of that one—other than standing and marching out. If they knew how she had gained the information, then in all probability Robin would be staying at home right beside her, his job gone for good. It was a thing that had never entered her mind until this moment. She had hardly noticed Robin's remark about the post not being advertised yet. She had done the whole thing in a fit of bravado. She couldn't even remember seeing the post advertised later.

The telephone suddenly rang, and she breathed a sigh of relief. A moment's respite. She tried to think fast, but never really got started, because one of the men picked it up and then glanced at the man in the shadows, the one that Catherine had been uneasily aware of all the time.

'Sorry. It's urgent.'

'Damn!'

Catherine glanced round, but she couldn't really see him until he actually stepped to the desk. She knew he was important by the way the others were looking at him, but it was not until he stepped into the sunlight

that she felt a wave of shock that went right through her
and down to her toes. Nobody had to tell her who it
was. The air of deference from her three tormentors told
her quite well. This was Damon King himself, and he
had been sitting there in the shadows watching. Her
'second sight' hadn't intrigued the others, it had intrigued Damon King. Her feeling of stepping into a hole
had been very good basic instinct.

She had never really imagined how he would look and,
if she had, her thoughts would not have painted the
splendid, aloof picture he made now. He looked what
he was—wealthy, secure and inflexible. There would be
no mercy from this man, and she knew it.

He had been comfortable while he watched and waited
too, as if she didn't matter. He had taken off the jacket
of his grey suit and unfastened the top button of his
shirt, loosening his tie, and now he leaned against the
desk and listened to the voice at the other end of the
phone.

'Foster and Brown?' He rapped out the name impatiently. 'Let them go. I'm not interested. Yes, I know
their turnover. It wouldn't be worth our while. Drop it.'

His voice was dark, like midnight velvet, alarming,
almost sinister, and it fitted exactly with what Catherine
had read about him. His face was harshly handsome,
utterly masculine, and his hair was dark—not the shining
jet of her own, but very dark all the same. She imagined
his eyes would be similar, but as he put the phone down
and turned towards her she got a further shock. His eyes
were tawny, amber, like some jungle cat, especially as
the sunlight slanted across them and turned them to burnished gold. She had never seen anyone quite like him.
His presence seemed to be dominating her.

He stared at her thoughtfully, saying nothing, his
strange eyes studying her face and hair, running over her
slim figure as if she were an object in a saleroom, and

she was surprised to find that he scared her; not many people did that. Her slender fingers clenched together, and he noticed immediately, glancing down at them before fixing her with his eyes again. He was summing her up, and it left her shaken, because everything was quite suddenly different. She had the feeling that something was terribly wrong, that she had been singled out. It was like walking into a waiting trap.

He went across for his jacket, shrugging into it while everyone seemed to wait spellbound for his decision, and Catherine couldn't take her eyes from him. Imagining him and being angry was one thing; actually seeing him was another. She knew now why people feared this man. He had an air about him that made him completely different from other people.

'That will do, gentlemen,' he said curtly, cutting the interview short with a glance at his awestricken tribunal. 'Follow me, Miss Farrell.'

His eyes fastened on her again and then he was walking to the door, tall and intimidating, holding it open for her and staring at her coldly as she approached. Her heart began to hammer, and she felt more nervous than she had ever felt in her life. Into the lion's den—unless he was about to throw her out into the street? She rather hoped he would.

In the lift she glanced at him secretly and looked away with some speed as she found those amber eyes still regarding her icily. Many times she had felt that she would like to attack this man, but now all she felt was defenceless. Danger seemed to be surrounding her, and she would have liked to be back with the other three, irritating though they were.

It was then that she remembered the last question. How had she known about the job? That was why she hadn't been thrown out yet. Damon King was going to get the information from her, and he looked as if he didn't much care how he went about it. That realisation changed her attitude and snapped her out of the peculiar feeling of fate. She would *not* be intimidated!

Her chin came up determinedly and her soft mouth set in one straight line. No way would he interrogate her! As she had no chance at all of this job, there was no possibility of his getting her to tell him about Robin. She looked determinedly into the cold-blooded, handsome face and saw amused boredom in the hard golden glitter of his eyes. He was evidently skilled at reading minds. It wouldn't do him a bit of good; she was determined on that.

As the lift doors swished smoothly open, he motioned her forward with extreme courtesy.

'My office. After you, Miss Farrell.'

His voice was nothing more than a low murmur, and Catherine looked round cautiously as she walked forward. They were much higher up in the great building now, surrounded by what appeared to be efficient luxury. It was a little isolated, and she wondered if there was any way of approaching other than by the lift. The trapped feeling grew, and as he opened a door for her and ushered her inside Catherine had the greatest urge to turn and run, to shout that she had changed her mind and make off as fast as possible.

As it was she never got the chance. He walked over to a huge desk and stood politely until she was seated in a facing chair. This time there was no sun in her eyes, and she almost wished it had been there. With the sun shining in her face she would not have been able to see him so well. He seemed at that moment to be a man greatly to be avoided, and Catherine's hands gripped together more tightly. Damon King was like a brilliant machine, and there was not one ounce of compromise in him. She was facing him head-on, and she could see no sign of anything but determination on his face.

He must have been well over six feet tall, and he looked exceptionally strong. He seemed to be totally in command of himself and everything else, very much at ease while she was dithering. She had never seen such a hard, handsome face before, and she could well understand why the business world feared him. Nobody had ever scared her in her life, but now she was holding her breath, and she knew it was because of the power he was transmitting. Her gauntlet had reduced itself to a limp rag.

'It was unfortunate that we were interrupted, Miss Farrell. We never did get an answer to that last question, did we?' He started right in with no pause, and Catherine took a steadying breath.

'I've quite forgotten what it was...' she began.

'In all the excitement,' he finished sardonically. 'Let me refresh your memory. How did you manage to write for an application form for the post of personal assistant to me, when we had not even advertised the vacancy?'

'Er—it was just on the off chance,' Catherine began with what she hoped was a careless shrug.

'Really? Most fortuitous. I may very well find you indispensable with your uncanny insight,' he murmured ironically. 'It's fascinating. All the time I've been imagining it was because you have a relative working here who picked it all up on the office grapevine. Or is Robin Farrell another coincidence?'

Catherine blushed wildly and then glared at him. There was, after all, no way of saving Robin from this man. She understood what George Darriel had meant about watching a train coming. She had nothing to lose at all now. The odd fear left her, so did her feeling of vulnerability, and she came out fighting.

'If you knew, then why waste your obviously valuable time in interrogating me?' she asked.

'I had hoped you would confess,' he assured her darkly, his eyes like two burnished stones. 'You're a big disappointment to me, Miss Farrell. As to your husband——'

'If you're referring to Robin, he's my brother,' Catherine cut in smartly. 'Your notes are less than reliable, Mr King.'

'I don't have notes,' he assured her quietly. 'I normally have no time to bother myself about smaller matters.'

'Like people?' Catherine fumed. 'I'm surprised you're bothering with me, then. I can't tell you anything that you don't already know, and as this interview has obviously been solely to bring trouble down on Robin's head I'll be very pleased to leave now.'

'As you wish, Miss Farrell.' He stood again with that absolutely infuriating courtesy, and it merely annoyed Catherine further. She felt she had made quite a fool of herself. Damon King had neither raised his voice nor shown any sign of annoyance. He almost seemed amused, and he probably was. It was no loss to him if she walked out, and he certainly knew where her information had come from.

'I hope you realise that my time is valuable too,' Catherine pointed out haughtily, pulling dignity around her. 'I could have spent this afternoon hunting for a job.'

'Now why would you do that?' He looked at her with mocking amusement. 'I imagined you were now my new personal assistant. We seem to have our wires crossed, Miss Farrell.'

CHAPTER TWO

'WHAT?' Catherine just stood and stared.

'You applied for the post. I assume you want it. Start on Monday, and Judith will get you settled in before she leaves.'

'Why?' Catherine whispered. Her throat felt dry, and she fully understood why he threw people into a panic. He was looking at her with no aggression—in fact his attitude was completely reasonable—but she was in trouble and she knew it.

'You're interesting.' His lips twisted sardonically. 'You might just prove to be useful.'

'As what?' Catherine was thrown completely off balance. Nothing was happening as she had expected, and there was a tremendous feeling of threat, as if she had no control over her own world.

'Time will tell, Miss Farrell. Meanwhile, you'll certainly astonish the opposition. Normally I would never contemplate taking on someone so young.'

'Suppose—suppose I can't...' All her confidence was fading, because this was impossible. She was quite sure that those three men in there had thought her utterly unsuitable, and if they had *he* did! He was the brains behind everything.

'If you can't,' he said silkily, 'we're looking at a very different situation. You got an interview by being in possession of information not available to other people. Office gossip is one thing; talking about it outside is quite another. Millions pass through these offices, paper transactions but all real. If your brother talks about one thing, he's likely to talk about other things, and we've had quite a few leaks of information lately. I might just have stopped the hole now I have you. Of course, if I *don't* have you, I can't really see any future for your brother. Let's say that you're a hostage for his good behaviour, shall we?'

Catherine just stared at him, mesmerised by cool golden eyes. He suspected Robin of betraying the firm and was quite prepared to dismiss him unless she stayed. It was blackmail!

'You can't do this! It's outrageous! Robin would never be dishonest. I only knew about this because we were chattering over a meal.'

'And how swiftly you acted,' he murmured, his eyes narrowed on her flustered face. 'With such a forceful sister he has quite an ally.'

'He doesn't need an ally, and if you believe that then surely you shouldn't employ me,' Catherine said quickly. If he suspected Robin, then taking on another suspect seemed like madness. Her own logic didn't quite take it in, but she knew how clever he was and she felt as if she were wriggling at the bottom of a net.

'You fit in with my plans.' He stared at her cynically for a minute. 'Let's have no more peculiarities, Miss Farrell. You applied for the post. Do you or do you not want it?'

Catherine just looked back at him desperately. Did she want the job? After his quiet threat she didn't have a lot of choice. Robin's future seemed to hang on her decision. There were no jobs available either, and even if there had been this was a priceless chance, the top of the tree. Whatever Damon King's dark reasons, she needed a job.

'Yes.' She said it worriedly, but he never gave any sign that he noticed.

'Very well. I'll see you some time in the future.' He dismissed her crisply and sat down, but Catherine still felt uneasy.

'What—what about the other people who applied for this post?' He had made her feel as if she had done something really wrong, when actually she had never even thought about it deeply, and now she was worrying about the injustice of all this.

'The post was never advertised.' He glanced up at her coldly, his voice curt. 'When you wrote for an application form for a vacancy that did not yet exist, the fact was brought immediately to my attention. It was obvious that somebody had been talking out of turn. We never advertised the post, therefore. It became very necessary to get *you*, Miss Farrell. I like my problems right in front of my nose, not hiding round the corner. If your brother has merely passed on the information about the vacancy, well and good. If that was just a small sample of his inclinations, however...'

He let the threat trail away into silence, and it was more alarming than any stated punishment.

'The lift will take you to the ground floor,' he murmured, turning away, his mind rapidly leaving her behind, and Catherine made her escape with as much speed as she could. She had got a job—a fabulous one— but she was frightened.

She knew too that he wouldn't keep her there for long. It was just because of Robin and the unreasonable suspicion that Damon King had. However short her time was with the King Group, it would be a time fraught with difficulties.

'You actually got it?' Robin exclaimed when she arrived home. Catherine had to tell him the bad part. She recounted the whole story except for the blackmail bit, and his face froze.

'He's got a nerve!' he snapped. 'I never even thought about the fact that nobody else knew. What about my future now?' he added angrily. 'That's the only reason I wanted you to work there. Things are worse than ever.'

'You could have been out of a job,' Catherine reminded him. '*That* would have been worse than ever. As it is, we're both safe for now, but there's no way I could approach him with any ideas about the record company. He would be sure to see something sinister in it. In fact, having seen him, I can't imagine him being at all interested in things like records.'

'That bit of the company makes money hand over fist,' Robin said bitterly. 'Of course he's interested. Anyway, it's his little toy, as you said.'

'He looks the sort of man who would have a dagger for a little toy,' Catherine pointed out uneasily. 'I can't sort it all out. He doesn't really want me for his PA. He doesn't like me and he'll never trust me. He doesn't trust you either. It's ridiculous. I mean, just because you mentioned the vacancy, there's no need for him to look upon you as a spy.'

'What do you mean?' Robin went quite pale, and she knew that he too feared Damon King. Still, who didn't? She explained carefully, and Robin was annoyed.

'Damned cheek!' he muttered. 'It's probably some deep trick of his. He's always up to something.'

But what trick? There was no way of knowing. What Catherine knew for sure was that she had met an intelligence of alarming proportions who used power like a sword, and she would never be able to work with him. She contemplated ringing up and refusing the job, but she was sure he would then ruthlessly sack Robin; he had as good as said so. And there was Gramps. There wasn't enough money for them all to live if she had no job and Robin was in the same fix.

Of course, Damon King might decide to get rid of her in the first week. She couldn't think of a single way he could fit her into any plans. She might have been a good PA, but she was absolutely lost at the thought of being one for him; she wouldn't dare make a single decision. He probably knew it too. He looked as if he did. His manner had been quite contemptuous, in spite of his alarming courtesy.

Catherine had the rest of the week and a whole weekend to work herself up into a panic about her unexpected job. It was preying on her mind every waking minute, but, true to her character, she decided to fill her time with things to do. Hard work was a good cure for most things. Her grandfather had taught both of them that from a very early age.

There was the garden to get ready, the house to clean, windows to polish, shopping to do. She went from one job to another and spent all her days keeping herself busy, trying not to think of the person she would have to meet on Monday.

There was Gramps, too. She had the feeling she would be much busier when she was working for the King Group, and her grandfather had to be left very safe and cosy. He read a lot and rang the library each week to order his favourite authors. Catherine always collected them for him, and on Friday that was exactly what she did, the last job she had to do for him before Monday loomed up.

She hurried along the pavement later, smiling to herself, her arms filled with books as she made her way home. Work had taken most of her worries away, and now she was looking forward to seeing her grandfather's pleasure. This time she had managed to get all the books he had ordered, and she knew they would last him all week.

Her beautiful face drew many admiring looks, but she never noticed. Her mind was on other things and she almost flew along, dodging people as she went, heading for the best place to get a taxi. She looked exotic with her red coat and her black hair, her skin glowing in the crisp air. For those few moments she hadn't a care in the world. Monday seemed a long way off.

She was going much faster that she realised, and a collision with a couple who came out of a shop was unavoidable. They stepped unexpectedly into her path, giving her no time to stop, and Catherine didn't even see them until it was too late. It was the man who bore the brunt of the impact, and the books flew from her arms, scattering all over the pavement, as she bumped into him.

She tried to keep her balance, but she was almost knocked off her feet, fully expecting to fall like the books until an arm like iron lashed round her waist, holding her fast. She was pulled securely against a hard male body that was as unyielding as rock, and her momentary feeling of safety disappeared fast as she looked up into two amber eyes that gleamed down at her mockingly.

'Why, Miss Farrell! Who are you running away from? If you'd warned me I could have helped you to escape. Are they still after you?'

Catherine felt a wave of strange awareness that quite shook her as Damon King continued to hold her tightly against him. She couldn't think of any reply. She just stared into his eyes like somebody trapped.

In the office with fairly familiar things around her she had felt this funny wave of feeling. Now she was pressed tightly to him and he was towering above her, obviously enjoying her shocked embarrassment. He was holding her deliberately close and people were beginning to look at them, but he seemed to be quite indifferent to passers-by.

'I—I'm sorry,' she managed shakily, not at all calmed when he gave a slight smile that hardly moved his lips. It was disparaging, mocking, leaving her in no doubt of his opinion of her. Now he thought she was an idiot as well as dishonest, and he still hadn't let her go.

'You were flying along with a smile on your face, Miss Farrell. Were you planning to skittle a few unwary passers-by, or did you actually *know* I was here?'

Catherine didn't really believe what he was implying—that she had set out to accost him for nasty reasons of her own. She just went on staring, and he seemed to take a delight in staring right back into her luminous grey eyes until she felt hypnotised.

'You should look where you're going,' a sharp voice said, and Catherine almost jumped, becoming aware that Damon King had not been alone. There was a smooth-looking blonde beside him, her eyes as hard as marbles, and Catherine's own words to Robin came back to her, about beautiful women falling over themselves to get to him. 'I'm glad she careered into you, darling,' the woman continued. 'At least you're strong enough to stand it.'

'You would have kept your footing, Leonie,' Damon murmured drily, still holding Catherine and watching her with glittering eyes. 'Miss Farrell is quite weightless, lighter than air, a creature of the clouds. It's her mind we have to worry about.'

'I'm sorry if I hurt you,' Catherine stammered, but the odd smile just broadened.

'Not even my dignity, Miss Farrell.'

That made matters worse. She didn't feel very dignified herself at the moment, and he obviously knew it. It was a minor catastrophe, and he was making it into a major one very deliberately. He was still holding her, and she hadn't even made a move to free herself; she couldn't!

He released her very slowly, and Catherine was so flustered that she didn't know where to look. She bent down quickly to retrieve the books, but he was bending down at the same time and she managed to bump her head into his. It wasn't very much, but it added to the feeling that she was behaving like a raving lunatic, and her cheeks felt hotter still.

'Allow me,' he murmured, crouching down and gathering the books. 'A few more incidents and you'll be irretrievably damaged. I don't think I could bear that.'

Catherine couldn't bring herself to stand and leave him to get the books. She couldn't very well fight him for possession of them either. She just stayed there, her black hair long and gleaming, hanging over her shoulder and halfway down her back. As she hadn't been at work she hadn't bothered to fasten it up, and even in the midst of his self-imposed task he glanced up at her keenly, his narrowed eyes skimming over her clear skin and shining hair.

Once again she just stared back, and his lips suddenly twisted wryly before he steadily gathered the scattered books.

'There.' He handed them to her, still crouched beside her, looking at her steadily, and Catherine felt a spark of anger adding to her disturbed feelings. She didn't know why he was doing this to her, but he was probably intending to behave like this all the time she was working for him. Maybe it was his idea of punishment for suspected crimes.

'Thank you.' She stood with one smooth movement, clutching the books. Her slight body poised angrily, her slender neck arched as she tossed back the long, gleaming hair. 'Once again I apologise; I'm *sure* it was entirely my fault.'

She couldn't keep the resentment out of her voice, and he looked extremely amused at the muted sarcasm.

She wanted to turn and walk away then, but he took her arm in a very strong grip.

'Do you need a taxi?' He stood looking down at her, his alarming eyes narrowed and assessing, and she was aware that his companion was fuming. He was just ignoring the other woman, presumably to cause further annoyance. Annoying people was probably another pastime for him, like Crown Records.

'I can get one myself, thank you,' Catherine assured him crisply, but he kept hold of her arm and stepped to the edge of the pavement. She hoped he would let go, because he seemed to have no idea how strong his grip was, and anyway, it took ages to get a taxi from this spot; that was why she had been going further along.

He raised his hand, and a taxi drew into the side of the pavement like magic. It was extremely vexing, and his eyes gleamed down at her, recognising her boiling irritation.

'Luck of the devil?' he enquired, almost in her ear. She didn't answer and he went on looking at her. 'I'll see you on Monday morning, Miss Farrell,' he said softly.

His tone had changed and the whole affair was suddenly quite threatening, as if one door had closed and another one opened. Every last drop of sardonic amusement had gone from his voice, and once again he was danger. He had deliberately made her very much aware of him. She was still flustered about being held so close, and everything had put her at a disadvantage. Now he was ready for the kill.

Catherine was anxious at once, her annoyance no longer a prop, and he smiled sceptically as she blurted out, 'Is everything all right?'

'What could be wrong? Everything is absolutely fine—unless I decide to sack both you and your brother, of course.'

Catherine bridled, her grey eyes filled with sparkling resentment. Her quick burst of fear left her rapidly at this challenge. She didn't threaten easily, and something like this, out in the open, she could deal with.

'There are other jobs! I'm sure we'd manage, Mr King.'

'And you would prefer to,' he announced. His lips turned down derisively. 'Perhaps you'll have to.'

'Then why did you bother to take me on in the first place, and why are you keeping Robin there?'

'Your brother isn't really important. You are. I told you, you fit into plans I have.' The golden eyes held hers, challenging still, but Catherine was too annoyed at that moment to take much notice.

'It's sure to be interesting, then. Everyone knows that you're a very hard businessman with plots hatching all over the place. I suppose I should feel flattered to be included in any plans you have!'

She stopped abruptly, suddenly realising what attitude she was taking, what he had goaded her into, and her cheeks flushed with embarrassment. He was a powerful, important man, and her new boss. He was also holding a sword over her head as far as Robin was concerned, and here she was, chastising him.

To her consternation he suddenly and very unexpectedly laughed.

'Don't apologise, Miss Farrell. I'm sure that's what you're about to do. I can see contrition on your face, but, believe me, I've enjoyed this encounter. I now feel I know you better, and I like to know my personal assistants. We'll probably end up being very close, don't you think?'

Catherine looked away quickly. She had been closer to him already than was safe and it still lingered in her mind; in fact she was shaking. She got hastily into the taxi, but he had already turned away, and she was very well aware that he had probably just been goading her to pass the odd boring minute.

Unless he really did have some awful plans. He still scared her. He had unashamedly used his masculinity to subdue her. There was the interview and now this. He intended to make her life miserable, and she knew that if she made one false move, or if Robin did, they were both out. It was cruel. She wondered just what she would have to stand in order to keep both her own job and Robin's.

When Catherine walked into the building on Monday morning there was a smartly dressed middle-aged woman waiting for her at the reception desk, and she came across, smiling pleasantly.

'Miss Farrell? I'm Judith Greaves; you're taking over my post.' At least here was a friendly face, Catherine thought thankfully as they went up in the lift together. Judith Greaves didn't speak on the way up, but there was a comfortable, warm feeling about her which transmitted itself to Catherine and made her feel temporarily safe.

'Have you been here a long time?' she asked.

'Oh, five or six years. I was with the Fenton Company before then. Mr King poached me.' She was laughing, and Catherine nodded. Yes, she could well imagine it, although he usually did his poaching in other directions, pulling in millions in the meantime. It was not surprising that if this woman had been good he would think nothing of poaching her from another firm where she was probably sorely missed.

'You must have felt very flattered,' Catherine suggested drily.

'Yes, I was actually. The company where I worked was rather slow—easygoing. I felt I wanted to get into a place where there was a bit more power.'

'Well, there's plenty of power with Mr King,' Catherine announced tightly, remembering with reluctance the feel of hard arms around her.

'There's certainly all of that.' Judith laughed. 'Anyway, I've enjoyed it here.'

'But you're getting married now?' Catherine wondered why Damon King had allowed this marriage at all. He seemed to be as autocratic as his name implied. She could well imagine him forbidding it.

'Oh, yes, second time around. Anyway, enough of gossiping about me; let's get you settled in. There's a lot to learn and not very much time.'

'When are you going?' Catherine felt as if she would like to cling on to this women for some considerable time. She needed to learn the ropes, and she definitely needed a shield against a certain man.

'Oh, three or four days. I'll stay as long as you need me. There's no real rush.'

They walked into an office very close to the one that Catherine had been in before. There was a communicating door into the great big office where Damon King had talked to her, and Catherine eyed it warily. She wondered if he was in there now. She was a bit bothered about facing him after Friday. Judith saw her glance and laughed.

'No, he's not in the building. In fact he's not in the building very often. He does a lot of work at home. He's got all the necessary equipment there, and with this modern technology he could work at home without ever coming into the office at all if he felt like it. From time to time, though, he comes in to keep us all on our toes.'

That didn't surprise Catherine at all. He probably came in and scared everybody to death.

'Of course, that's why I'm always here,' Judith went on. 'He needs somebody here all the time, and I'm usually sitting in for him. Even if he worked at the office he spends hours at meetings and travels a good deal. There's plenty for his assistant to do. We'd better get started.'

Relieved to know there was no man in the office to keep her on edge, Catherine set to with a will. She was clever, very eager, and picked things up quickly. At the end of the day Judith was congratulating her.

'You know the ropes pretty much already.'

'But don't leave me,' Catherine begged quickly.

'No, a couple more days.' Judith laughed. 'In any case, there's really nothing to worry about.'

That was what *she* thought! Catherine knew exactly what she was worrying about.

She was much more settled in her mind when she went home that night, though. If she could just get her foot under the table before Damon King came in at all she would be feeling quite pleased with herself. She would be more able to tackle him. Not that he would need tackling, she quickly reminded herself. She had better remember she was working for him, and under a certain amount of threat.

Robin looked at her a bit anxiously as she came in. 'How did it go?'

'Perfectly well. Judith Greaves is very nice. I get on well with her. It's a pity she's not staying and *him* going.'

'The firm would collapse without him,' Robin assured her. 'He's the man who makes the wheels go round. I've been looking over my shoulder all day, expecting him to come in.'

'I hear he doesn't come in often.'

'No. When he does you never know he's there until you suddenly look up. People shudder about the way he looks. He's never even looked at me.'

'Let's hope he doesn't in the future,' Catherine said earnestly, remembering Damon King's suspicions.

Her grandfather looked a bit better today, and
Catherine breathed a sigh of relief. Her first day was
over, she had got on very well with Judith Greaves, Robin
was quite subdued, not mentioning a word about his
future career, and her grandfather looked all right. It
couldn't have been such a bad day after all.

The bad day came on Wednesday. Judith was to leave
at lunchtime. She was quite satisfied in her mind that
Catherine was settled and knew all she would have to
know for the time being. All morning people were
popping into the office to leave little presents for Judith.
She had obviously been very popular, and Catherine
watched and learned a lot about the people in the firm
and their attitude. She got on with her own jobs quietly.
It would have been nice if Damon King had come in to
say goodbye, she thought. He was probably above that
sort of thing. He went down another notch in her
opinion, although there wasn't very far for him to go.

She met one of the chief accountants too. Gordon
Turner came in to say goodbye to Judith, and she introduced him to Catherine. She had done that with all
of them, but they had obviously been quite keen to leave
in case the tiger stalked in. Gordon Turner stayed to talk.
Evidently he was not as easily intimidated as the others.

'You can't be old enough for this job,' he stated,
looking at her admiringly.

'I am.' Catherine laughed. 'I have the feeling I'll be
much older after a week here with Judith gone.'

'Call down to me,' he offered with a grin. 'I'll protect
you from the boss.' He stayed a while longer, and
Catherine liked him. He was not in any way threatening,
and she was beginning to appreciate men who looked as
if they would be kind and easy to get on with. She was
about to work with a man who looked as if he would
gobble her up for doing very little wrong. He almost had
done already.

Just before lunchtime an enormous flower arrangement was delivered to Judith, and she blushed with pleasure.

'It's from Mr King,' she said. 'How typical.'

There was a long envelope attached, and when Judith opened it Catherine saw a cheque inside.

Judith's eyes opened wide. 'Oh, this is too much,' she gasped.

She looked quite overwhelmed, and Catherine ventured, 'It would have been rather nice if he'd come in to give it you himself.'

'He doesn't do things like that,' Judith murmured, still staring at the cheque and flowers. 'He does his good by stealth.'

'I didn't know he did any good at all,' Catherine muttered.

Judith looked at her strangely.

'He's a rather complicated man; you'll have to work really hard to get to know him. And he *does* do good by stealth. I've never known him do anything that was bad, anyway.'

'What about all the firms he absorbs?'

'That's business, my dear, and he's a very good businessman. He has been since he was very young, apparently.' Judith looked at her levelly. 'You don't like him do you?'

'I—I don't know him,' Catherine managed hastily. She felt as if she had been speaking out of turn, perhaps a little disloyally, and that was a new feeling in any case. She had staunch ideas about loyalty, but it would be stretching things to extend them to Damon King.

'Well, as I say, he's a complicated character but very easy to get on with once you know how his mind works.'

That was something she would never know, Catherine decided. How could an ordinary person know how Damon King's mind worked? It was going to be difficult enough just keeping out of trouble, without psycho-analysing the boss.

When Judith had gone Catherine had the office to herself, and she gave a little shudder that was partly fright but mostly pleasure. She had never felt high-powered before, and it was rather a good feeling.

She walked across and looked out of the window. The towering building looked over the city. There was a little park opposite, and the trees were already green with the foliage of springtime, but somehow she didn't feel trapped up here now. Everything would be quite all right just so long as Damon King never came into the office.

He confounded her by walking in at that very moment. He just came straight through her door without going into his own office, and Catherine had the feeling that he had come in deliberately to take her by surprise. As she was standing gazing out of the window he had succeeded very well, and she felt guilty.

'Business slack, is it, Miss Farrell?' He looked across at her with a sort of hard mockery, and Catherine decided to stand her ground. She hadn't seen him since the book episode, so there was a certain amount of embarrassment on her face, but she had to squash it. This was her new boss, somebody she would have to see frequently. She might as well get used to facing him right now.

'At the moment, but I'm sure everything is under control.'

'Oh, I never thought it wouldn't be with you here.'

He didn't say another word. He just slanted her an ironic glance and went through to his own office, and she knew he had merely come in to upset her, just as he had held her tightly to upset her. If all this punishment was because he suspected Robin, then it just wasn't fair. Deep down she knew he suspected her too, but she refused to think about it.

She gave a little sigh and sat down at her own desk. The phone rang and she was back to business very quickly, the thought of Damon King drifting out of her mind, even though he was just next door. She was left with a hazy feeling that he was on an entirely different plane from herself. An unreachable man. Not that she wanted to reach him!

She couldn't really believe he had any plans for her. If he had been trying to frighten her he had certainly succeeded at the time, but now she had herself settled in. The salary was going to be very welcome at home, and Robin was still in a job. Things couldn't be very bad after all.

It was nearly time to leave before she even heard a sound from Damon's office, and then he called her through. When she went in he was sitting at his desk, his hands flat on the top, his golden eyes already staring at her as she walked through the door.

'Sometimes, Miss Farrell, I shall want you to work away from the office,' he said without preamble, and Catherine felt an instant stab of anxiety.

'Where exactly?' she asked, trying to sound quite sure of herself. She had just been feeling safe, and now she was worried again. It was only when she was actually facing him that she remembered how overwhelming he was.

He leaned back and looked at her steadily.

'I work at home quite a lot. I'll want you to work there with me.'

Instantly Catherine panicked. This was the last thing she had expected, and she knew he was up to yet more mischief.

'Judith Greaves didn't work there!'

'No, Judith didn't work there, but you're different.'

'How?' Catherine asked breathlessly. 'Why am I different? I'm just your personal assistant. It's the same.'

'Not quite. You have attributes that Judith did not have,' he said silkily.

What attributes? She couldn't think of even one—unless . . . ! She looked at him suspiciously and he looked back at her with no expression on his face at all. Of course not. She worked hard at calming herself. He didn't need to trick a woman; they fell over themselves to get to him, and he didn't even like her anyway. The way he had held her when she bumped into him had been deliberate, aimed at scaring her. She wasn't going to be scared again, even if he was black all the way through.

'Is it far away?' she asked brightly, looking him in the eye.

'Not too far. I'll transport you—unless you're staying there.'

The last was a quiet murmur, and Catherine could see an expression growing at the back of his eyes that looked like amusement. She abandoned subterfuge rapidly.

'*Staying* there?'

He merely raised dark eyebrows at her horrified question. 'Of course. I don't come in every day myself, and I really need you to work with me. Transporting you back and forth would be ridiculous.'

He was taking an attitude, she noticed, behaving as if she were stupid to be suspicious. Well, it wouldn't work.

'Who will watch the office?' she asked triumphantly. That would stop him easily! Watching the office was *her* job. She had to sit in for him. Judith Greaves had said so.

'Miss Farrell, there are plenty of people here to watch the office and, in any case, when I'm working at home and this office is unoccupied all calls are switched directly to me. I imagine the office will survive without you,' he finished drily.

'I see.' At the moment she couldn't really think of a way out of this—other than saying, 'No!' very loudly.

'Do you?' he murmured wryly. 'I hope you do. In any case, as I pointed out when we first met, I want you for wider plans. Judith would never have been suitable.'

There was a gleam in his eyes that told her he was laughing at her, but he said nothing else. He simply nodded to her, murmured goodnight, and walked out, and Catherine was left staring after him worriedly. This was something she had never anticipated. She felt on the edge of danger again, and she realised he had never asked her if she was willing to go. He had quietly issued a command. It was above and beyond the call of duty as far as she could see, but she was still facing the blackmail. Both her own job and Robin's depended on her co-operation. Once again, she had no choice.

CHAPTER THREE

CATHERINE didn't tell Robin. They had arranged to go home together, and he was particularly silent, so she decided not to add to any anxieties he had already.

'Is anything wrong?' she asked finally, trying to push her own worries to the back of her mind.

'I've been wondering about packing it all in,' he said after a moment's hesitation. 'You've got a good job now.'

'Packing it all in? To do what?' Catherine looked bewildered, but he was staring grimly ahead.

'I've been wondering about taking a chance—just launching out into music with a bang.'

'Robin, you can't do it on your own! Where are you going to get your backing from?'

'I don't know; I haven't thought it out completely yet, but there are plenty of things I could do. I could travel all over the country, entertaining at clubs and places, for one thing. That would be a start.'

'Oh, Robin.' Catherine stared at him in exasperation. 'We've been through all this before, and you know perfectly well you wouldn't be happy doing that. It's not the sort of thing you should be doing.'

'Because you want me to be an accountant.'

'I don't want you to be anything but happy, Robin.' She sounded weary, and he relented, putting his arm around her shoulders.

'I know. You're a very motherly little thing.'

'I'm a year younger than you,' Catherine said sharply, and he grinned to himself.

'I know it, but I often wonder if you do. I suppose, being the only woman in the house, you feel like a mother and maiden aunt all rolled into one.'

'Well, you take some looking after!' They were both laughing, and Catherine felt a wave of relief. It was just his frustration coming out. He wouldn't do anything foolish.

'How did you get on today?' Robin asked.

'Very well. Judith Greaves left. She got a cheque and a big flower arrangement from Damon King. In fact when she went home her arms were full of parcels. The people in the office seem nice.'

'They are.'

'Then why don't you want to stay?' Catherine pounced immediately.

'You know why, Cath. I've got talent and I'm going to push it, no matter what it takes.'

She nodded; she had the nasty feeling that he would. Her relief had been short-lived.

'I hope you won't simply walk out without a penny to your name,' she persisted worriedly. 'We won't be able to help you. Even though I'll be getting a good salary now, if you're not earning it will take all that to run the house, and we've got to be able to make sure that Gramps has what he needs. He's looked after us, and he's old now.'

'I know, I know,' he said soothingly. 'Don't worry about me. If I decide to take off I'll be fairly well-heeled.'

'But how?' She knew perfectly well he had next to nothing in the bank.

'I've made a few plans.' He sounded deliberately mysterious, and Catherine's soft lips tightened.

'Now look here, Robin——' she began, but he interrupted her sharply.

'No, *you* look, Cath. You may feel like my big sister, but you're nothing of the sort. I know exactly what I'm

doing, and when I decide to take off I'll make sure you
and Gramps are comfortable. I'll also have plenty of
money. I'll be able to wait until I get my big chance
then.'

Catherine shook her head and decided to let the matter
drop, because there was no way he could get any big
money—and that was what he was implying. If he left
there was her own job to consider too. With no hold
over Robin, Damon King would have no use for her. She
had enough problems right now, without anything new.

Over the next couple of weeks Catherine settled into her
job. The more demanding work was bringing out the
best in her, and she found to her great joy that she was
very capable. She just hoped it would continue and that
nothing would happen to mar the smooth working days.
As to going to Damon King's house, she put that firmly
to the far back of her mind. It just wasn't going to
happen, because he had never mentioned it again.

When he was there he was polite and distant, working
with her whenever it was necessary, but he always gave
her a breathless feeling which she was sure was fear. She
would sometimes look up and find his eyes running over
her in a speculating manner, and when her grey eyes
challenged him he just looked cynically amused, as if it
was some sort of game.

When he came in on Friday at the end of her first two
weeks she thought things were normal, until he called
her into his office and said, 'When you come in on
Monday morning, Miss Farrell, please come prepared
to stay away for a few days.'

Catherine felt drawn back into the black cloud of
anxiety.

'To stay away?' she asked slowly. She was watching
him like a trapped animal, and it didn't please him.

'We've been through this once,' he pointed out sharply. 'For the past two weeks I've come into the office to help you settle in. Now I wish to carry on my normal way of working. My normal way of working is at home. I shall need you.'

'But——'

'No buts, Miss Farrell.' He was looking at her icily now. 'I work from home and, beginning on Monday, you will be working there with me for a while. Pack a suitcase for about two weeks.'

Catherine's heart sank. Two weeks locked up with him. She didn't know if she was going to survive it.

'I—I've got commitments at home,' she stammered.

'I'm quite sure your brother is capable of looking after himself. He's older than you. There's no need for you to mother him.'

'I don't mother him, but you see there's my grandfather.'

He leaned back in his chair and looked at her steadily, his cold expression easing slightly, although he did look as if he thought it might be a ploy to get her out of things.

'He lives with you?'

'No, actually we live with him, Robin and me—he brought us up.'

'I see!'

'You don't really see, Mr King. My grandfather's an old man now and he's not terribly well. I suppose Robin could look after him. We've had to leave him while we've gone out to work each day. He'll probably be all right, but...' She was very hesitant, and he was watching her closely. Most nights Robin was out at some club or other, performing. Sometimes at the weekends he was away in an entirely different place and didn't come home at all. She wasn't sure how they could manage it. She knew, though, that if she refused to go she was going to lose this job. Robin would surely lose his job too.

'I didn't realise you had problems,' Damon said finally, after watching her in silence. 'How are you going to get out of it?'

'I suppose I could get someone to call round and look at him.'

'Look at your grandfather? Is he in bed?'

'No. He wouldn't like it either.' She smiled ruefully and shook her head. 'He doesn't like people looking after him.'

'I can imagine. Just because he's old I don't suppose it makes him any less of a man.'

'No. I expect he'll be all right. Robin will be there. After all, lots of old people just stay by themselves—don't they?'

'They do. Let's see how it goes, shall we?'

'Yes.' She was surprised how kind he seemed to be just at that moment, and she gave him a startled look. Their eyes locked. He was almost smiling. The first time he had ever done that—in any nice sort of way.

'I—I'll pack a bag for two weeks, then,' Catherine said hurriedly. 'I could ring my grandfather every day, I suppose?'

'Of course you could. You'll just be working in a different place. I don't intend to imprison you, Miss Farrell.'

She didn't know if that was a joke or not. He still had the strange smile on his face. She would never be able to reckon him up. Maybe, working closer to him at his house, she would be able to understand him a bit more. She almost shook herself. She didn't want to understand him. What was she saying? He was just the man she worked for, and a very awkward man at that.

When she told her grandfather, he looked very annoyed and suspicious.

'Going to work at his house? What sort of a man is he?'

'He's very cool and—er—respectable,' Catherine said quickly, not quite sure of that last fact.

'You watch him. He might turn out to be a villain, and you're a very beautiful girl.'

'Oh, Gramps, I'm his personal assistant! It's not unusual for businessmen nowadays to work from home. With modern technology it's easy and more convenient——'

'Never you mind,' he interrupted gruffly. 'You make sure you phone me every single day.'

'I've already arranged that, but will you be all right?'

'What do you mean? Of course I'll be all right!' He was quite stroppy, and she remembered what Damon King had said about making her grandfather feel less of a man. He was quite right after all. Her grandfather was still a force to be reckoned with, and she felt easier in her mind.

They were having tea when Robin came in. She had not come home with him tonight. He had been working late for some reason, and she had left him to it.

'I've got news,' she said cheerfully. 'I'm going away for a fortnight.'

'He's giving you a holiday already?' Robin looked sceptical, and Catherine shook her head.

'No, he's not. As you probably know, he works from home a lot. I'm to go there and work with him.'

Robin's reaction was instantly like that of her grandfather. His face darkened and he glared at her.

'What for?' He was quite truculent, and Catherine tried not to laugh. She felt responsible for these two men, but in actual fact she realised now that they both felt the need to protect her.

'He needs his PA to work with him at home. He's got everything there he needs. Apparently he works from home a lot—you must know that.'

'I know! Everyone does. They also know that he didn't take Judith Greaves home with him.'

'Well, he must be changing his work habits.' Catherine tried to make it all sound matter-of-fact, because her grandfather was looking very suspicious again. 'Anyway, I expect he has a house full of servants,' she added, with a burst of inspiration.

'Naturally he would,' Robin said a trifle sourly. 'He's rolling in money. I don't expect he scrubs his own floors.'

It seemed to quieten their fears, and Catherine felt she had had some sort of an escape. She could not do with these two clucking over her. She had quite enough to do dealing with her new boss.

She was in the office in good time on Monday morning, and Damon was waiting for her. It gave her the feeling that he was gathering her in like some prey, but she couldn't think what he expected her to do wrong. At the back of her mind, though, she knew exactly what he expected. He thought she could steal information from the firm, sell it to other people. He probably imagined she was in league with Robin. Neither of them would even know where to begin, even if she had the information, which she most certainly had not.

She was used to confidentiality and quite angry at the thought that he was keeping her tightly to her side, as if he intended to watch her constantly. She shot him a very annoyed look, and his dark brows rose.

'You want to back out at the last minute, Miss Farrell?' he asked tightly.

'Of course not!' Catherine gave him a small scowl.

'Then let's go.' He took her case and walked off, and she was left with no alternative but to trot behind him.

Several people they passed as they went through the very large foyer looked very speculatively at her, and it made her more irritable than ever. She had no idea what they were thinking, but she could guess, and she supposed that the chairman of the King Group rarely carried anyone's suitcase about for them. He seemed to be intent on ruining her reputation, and he was starting right here. Now she was going to be suspected of other things besides business espionage.

The house was well outside London, and as the powerful car turned into the long, tree-lined drive Catherine looked at Damon's face. This was his domain where no one intruded. She had not wanted to be anywhere near him, and now she was being carefully driven to his own private kingdom.

The drive curved inwards, and then she saw the house—not the modern house she had imagined, but an Elizabethan manor house unexpectedly tucked away in this area of tranquillity. It was the pleasing dark red brick of its period, with tall chimneys silhouetted against the sky, and the gardens around it adding to the feeling of peace.

'Oh!' Catherine breathed. She had not expected anything like this, in spite of his wealth.

'Ravenhall Manor,' Damon announced quietly, 'or, to follow local custom, simply Ravenhall. I hope you'll feel comfortable enough to work here.'

Catherine never answered. She was too busy feasting her eyes. She had been dreading this, but now she could hardly wait to get inside and look around. She was utterly entranced.

He stopped the car and came round to open the door for her.

'It's beautiful,' she said in an awed voice as he looked down at her.

'Thank you, Miss Farrell. I like it.'

'Please . . .' Catherine looked up at him with a certain amount of pleading in her eyes. She didn't want this spoiled, and he was cold as ice. It seemed terribly important that they get on a better footing. It would be dreadful to work with a cold, hard man every day. 'As I'm working here and I'll be seeing you all the time, do you think you could do what my other boss did?'

'And what was that? Nothing too alarming, I hope.'

'He called me by my first name.' Catherine felt her face flush, and he instantly relented, dropping his taunting manner.

'I'll give it a try. I want you to be happy. I need you here.'

As far as she could see there was no choice at all, happy or not. He had ordered her to come. Still, this place looked like paradise. It would be easy to be happy here. She felt a pang of guilt when she thought about her grandfather, but she couldn't look after him all the time and she would ring him every day—and see him at the weekend probably. It was only two weeks.

She suddenly realised she was still sitting in the car and that Damon was standing outside with his hand on the door, waiting for her to get out. She looked up. His eyes were narrowed on her as if he was trying to pick up her thoughts—and then she saw a quirk to his lips that meant he was probably assuring himself that she was some sort of an idiot again.

She got out very quickly—almost falling in her haste to get past him—and they were almost at the front door when it opened and a woman stood there, watching, a smile on her face.

'This is my housekeeper, Mrs Jarvis,' Damon introduced.

'You must be Miss Farrell,' the woman said. 'Mr King told me he would be bringing his assistant home. I must say I didn't expect anyone so young.'

'Neither did I, Mrs Jarvis,' Damon said mockingly, and Catherine hurried after him as he walked inside with her case. She would have liked to spend a few minutes chatting to the housekeeper, but he would not want to feel that she was already getting her foot in as if she were part of the household. The house was beautiful, but she was only here to work.

The downstairs rooms were oak-panelled, glowing in the sunlight, there was a high gleam on the parquet floor, and a round table in the middle of the hall held an old brass bowl filled with flowers. There was a gallery supported by oak beams, and the stairs were at the side. Everything was perfect.

They went into a large drawing-room with soft lights set into the panelling. The chairs and settees looked softly comfortable and the colours were warm and glowing. There was a French window that looked out on to the garden. It was late April now and things were just beginning to bloom, the high banks of rhododendrons and the cherry trees just showing blossom.

It was a wonderful place. It was hard to imagine that Damon chose to live here. Her imagination had placed him in some starkly modern apartment right in the city, and she wondered what his girlfriend thought about it.

Her mind went back to that woman with the blonde hair. Still, she probably came from a similar background and was used to this sort of thing—she could easily get used to it herself. Catherine sighed, and Damon was just coming in.

'Bemoaning your fate?' he asked ironically.

'I was just thinking how beautiful it is here,' she said in a quiet voice, but he didn't look as if he really believed that.

'I wondered if you were wishing yourself miles away.'

'No, it's lovely.' For the first time she turned her brilliant eyes on him and smiled. 'I was wishing it were mine, actually.'

He looked at her intently and then laughed.

'Were you? Enjoy it while you can, then.'

Mrs Jarvis came in with a tray of tea, and Catherine had no time to consider what he had meant by that last remark. It had the air of threat about it, though, as if she was already condemned.

His housekeeper looked very motherly. Her smile was warm, and she didn't look particularly in awe of Damon. But then he didn't suspect Mrs Jarvis of anything. It was a pity about his attitude. It was wonderful here, and he was going to spoil it. Still, she would try to get round him. She smiled to herself as Mrs Jarvis left, and when she looked up Damon was watching her, his eyes intently on her face.

'Panic over?' he asked quietly.

'I never panic,' Catherine informed him in a very worldly voice, and his lips quirked with amusement. Whatever his real motives were in bringing her here, she could see he intended to get the maximum enjoyment out of her stay, and it cancelled out any feeling of contentment.

She drank her tea and kept her eyes averted, but really she would have liked to watch him and sum him up— he always seemed to be doing that to her. She didn't quite have the nerve, though.

'Let's hope you fit into the smooth running of things,' he murmured, and Catherine looked up quickly, wondering what his latest comment meant and how many more of them there were going to be.

'You'll find me quiet and perfectly house-trained,' she said defiantly. 'I'll be sure to remember that I'm not a guest.'

'You certainly know how to stick up for yourself, don't you?' he growled. He gave her a long, considering look. 'I hope I don't get myself into a situation where I have to watch my tongue—it would be an entirely new experience for me.'

'I don't expect I'll see you much,' Catherine said quickly, realising she was stepping very close to the mark with him. At this rate he would sack her today, Robin too. 'I'll just get on with my work and you won't see much of me at all.'

'Don't bank on that. I intend to see a lot of you.' He just stared at her with those amber eyes until she looked down. 'How old are you, Catherine—twenty-four?'

'Yes.' She looked up again, surprised he had wondered about it. 'There's not quite a year between Robin and me.'

'Hmm!' He was still staring at her rather fixedly. 'Your brother is very good at his job.'

'I don't suppose you'd employ him if he weren't.' Catherine almost blurted out that he was rather good at doing other things too—playing the guitar and singing—but she remembered just in time and kept quiet. 'It's a lovely garden,' she improvised, changing the subject quickly. Speaking of her brother annoyed him. She could tell that clearly. Damon's eyes slanted across to look through the French window.

'I don't often get the chance to enjoy it,' he said shortly. 'It's private here. That's enough.'

'I expect you enjoy it at the weekend,' Catherine ventured, feeling an urgent need to make polite conversation and occupy his mind.

'I'm usually too busy.' She didn't know exactly what he meant, but her mind went back to that woman he had been with, and although she had not read anything particular about his private life she did know that he had a certain reputation with ladies.

Mrs Jarvis came in and smiled across at them.

'I've taken your suitcase up to your room, Miss Farrell. If you'd like to follow me I'll show you where it is.'

Catherine was glad to get out. Damon stood politely as she left, and she was well aware that his eyes followed her from the room. She was never going to stop feeling nervous with him. She straightened her shoulders and tried to pretend it didn't matter, but really it mattered very much. She followed Mrs Jarvis up the stairs and could not help looking round to see if he was standing watching her. To her great relief he was not.

Her bedroom looked out over the gardens at the front, and it was another place she wanted to stay indefinitely. The white ceiling had dark narrow beams across it, and the long casement window was draped in curtains to match the cover of the bed. She was quite intrigued by the bedhead—it appeared to be hand-painted—and Mrs Jarvis smiled at her interest.

'That's Italian and quite old,' she informed Catherine. 'In fact I think it's very old indeed, but so delicate. Mr King found it while he was abroad and had it brought back here.'

It was a strange shade of white, almost tinted, and the flowers were delicate and brilliantly coloured. The dressing-table and chest of drawers were a matching shade, and Catherine could see that they had been carefully tinted to fit in with the headboard. Damon had beautiful taste, whatever his manner was. Even the pictures blended in with the room. Mrs Jarvis went out, and after a second, while she was wandering around admiring the room, Catherine looked up to find Damon standing in the doorway watching her.

'Are you happy with your room?'

Catherine turned to the window and looked down, anxious to escape from the probing eyes.

'Who wouldn't be? It's lovely. I've never slept in a room like this before.'

'You sound like a pleased little girl. I wonder if you're as guileless as you seem?' He walked further into the room and stared down at her. 'Women are astute creatures, skilled at playing the innocent. I can't quite decide about you, though.'

'It's no use asking me to tell you,' Catherine pointed out solemnly. 'You wouldn't believe me.'

'No. I wouldn't.' He went on looking at her and then turned impatiently away. 'You've got a good view of the garden from here. My room is at the back of the house, with equally pleasant views but not so much garden. You seem to be greatly taken with the place.'

'I help my grandfather with the garden at home,' Catherine said quietly. She turned to look out of the window. It was a good excuse to look away. She was very aware that he was standing close. These feelings that he provoked were new to her—being aware that she was in close proximity to a powerful male. She was well aware that his actions when he had held her fast had brought it on, but it took very little to bring the feeling back again now.

She wanted to edge away. It would not do to be physically aware of a man like Damon King. It would just be asking for trouble. Her face flushed at the thought and she glanced at him worriedly, but he was looking out over the garden now, his face rather set, and he suddenly looked down at her sharply.

'What else do you do, other than being an ideal granddaughter and devoted sister?'

'I'm like anyone else.' Catherine flushed painfully at his taunt, and he turned away abruptly.

'I'm beginning to doubt it. Lunch will be served soon. Come down when you're ready.'

Catherine watched him walk out. She didn't understand his new attitude at all. If he thought she was guileless he could hardly think she was prepared to steal vital information too. She was very glad when he closed the door behind him.

Immediately after lunch they started work. Catherine had a small room across the hall from Damon's study, and it had obviously been a sitting-room. When Damon informed her that he had had some things moved out and a desk put in for her, it brought home once again that this was an unusual arrangement—specifically for her. She was to be close to him so that he could watch her. She would be suspected constantly, and the knowledge was distressing.

Everything was simply being put through to Ravenhall Manor. Damon was in residence, and the whole firm had swung round towards him. By late afternoon Catherine was quite settled and very pleased to go off to her own beautiful room when Damon announced that they had finished. Things had gone much better than she had expected, and she hadn't seen a lot of him.

When she went down to dinner Mrs Jarvis had placed her quite close to Damon, and Catherine wasn't sure whether she liked that. She was not sure either whether she would have liked to be sitting at the end of the table with him staring at her down its length.

'You lived through the first day,' Damon pointed out wryly when she gave him a worried look.

'Yes. I've enjoyed it,' Catherine confessed. While she had been in her room she had been thinking about phoning her grandfather. It was nearly eight o'clock now and he would be rather worried.

'So what went wrong?' He had obviously concluded that she had a problem.

'I was just wondering about phoning my grandfather.'

'Go ahead, immediately you've eaten, or even before.'

'There isn't a phone in my room.'

He smiled ironically.

'An oversight, I'm sure. Let's see how long you stay before we get round to that. There's a phone in your study, one in mine, one in the hall and one in the drawing-room.'

'I didn't mean to be critical...'

'Are you ever? I'll see you get privacy, if that's the problem. Use your own office phone.' The hard mockery had dropped away and he was simply looking amused. Catherine tried to look businesslike.

'Thank you. I'll do it straight after dinner.'

They ate in silence for a while and then Damon said, 'Tell me about your grandfather.'

'He brought us up.' Catherine didn't know what else to say. She was sure he would not be interested in her grandfather and was just making polite conversation. He persisted, however.

'What happened to your parents?'

'They died, very soon after each other. There was only my grandfather then. I suppose you think that makes us a very small family.'

'Bigger than some families. You're not on your own, at any rate. How old were you?'

'Seven. Robin was eight. I hardly remember now. Gramps has always been wonderful to us. He's dealt with our peculiarities.'

'Even though I think you're an oddity, perhaps other people don't,' Damon murmured drily. 'You're an oddity in my world. Maybe you're normal in your own.'

'I'm normal in any world,' Catherine insisted, looking at him levelly. 'You give me credit for gifts I don't possess, like deceit.

She saw an expression flash across his face that was not pleasant, and she wished she had never spoken. He had not forgotten why he had her here. She was chatting away to him, telling him things about herself. She had better watch her step.

'I didn't think you'd be here tonight.' Catherine spoke into the suddenly uncomfortable silence, and he looked up at her quizzically.

'And where did you think I would be?'

'I imagined you'd have a glamorous life.' Once again Catherine wished she had held her tongue, but, as usual with her, it was too late.

'Glamorous?' He laughed rather harshly. 'Busy, perhaps. Glamorous? Not really.'

She stared at him for a minute, remembering that she had never, ever read anything about his past. It was if he had sprung from some other place and just started at about twenty-five. At any rate, he didn't look lonely. He just looked icily self-assured. Even his quirks of humour had the edge of cruelty, but he was always wonderfully polite, and that in itself was an armour, she realised.

She looked up and he was watching her. He was leaning back in his chair, his glass in his hand, and an odd smile was playing along his lips.

'You can dispense with the disguise, Catherine,' he ordered softly, and she looked at him with puzzled eyes. She hadn't the faintest idea what he was talking about. His lips twitched at her expression.

'Very appealing,' he congratulated. 'Not necessary, though. I'm talking about your hair.' She had kept it up all day and it was swept to the top of her head now, her slender neck poised above the sage-green dress she wore. 'Now you have the job,' he continued, 'there's no need to maintain the sharp woman-of-the-world disguise. You can let that glorious hair down. I'll even give you permission to be yourself.'

'I'm not trying for any disguise,' Catherine protested, blushing furiously. She was, and she knew it. She was much more comfortable with her long hair around her shoulders.

'Then indulge me,' he murmured drily. 'I rather think you were more normal when we met so precipitately in London.'

He didn't need to mention the fact that he had held her closely then; it was all there in the amused expression deep in his eyes.

'I don't go around knocking people over,' she pointed out. 'If you think that's normal, though——'

'I think normal for you was when you were racing along with a smile on your face, a pile of books in your arms,' he said softly. 'Now that you're not in the office you can relax. There's just you and me, nobody to pretend for.'

Catherine was glad when Mrs Jarvis came in at that moment to tell him there was a phone call. It gave her the chance to escape. If he thought her rude, he would just have to make the best of it. At the moment she couldn't face him, because his words had sunk in after only a second.

She had not bumped into him accidentally. He had seen her coming along the pavement, and therefore he could easily have avoided the collision. And what had he meant by saying there was nobody to pretend for? Again, it rather sounded as if he had already condemned her.

When she phoned her grandfather later she also had a word with Robin. Everything was going well at their end, and they were very interested to find out that she had a comfortable study to work in and that it was a most beautiful house. She realised later that she had talked more about the house than anything else. It left her going to bed with a very strange feeling, as if she had stepped into another world—a world she did not particularly want to get out of at the moment.

CHAPTER FOUR

RIGHT from the first Catherine felt a strange kind of happiness at Ravenhall. She was never intimidated for long—her nature was much too buoyant for that—and, as the days went by, the possibility that Damon had something unpleasant planned for her became much more unlikely. In any case, she had been brought up by her grandfather to look on the bright side, and the instinct was too deeply ingrained to cast away.

Judith Greaves had told her that Damon was away at meetings a lot and that he spent a great deal of time overseas, but in that first week he did neither of those things. He was around the house all the time and, although he was in his study and she hardly saw him unless there was some consultation to do, she was well aware that he was there.

She knew he was keeping an eye on her, or at least she assumed so, but she shrugged the idea off. If he wanted to waste his time keeping any eye on somebody who was about to do absolutely nothing unusual, then that was his affair. All she wanted was to keep her job and work in the peace of this house.

On Friday she was really looking forward to going home for the weekend. Damon had not said that she would have the weekend off, but she assumed so. Robin had a car, and she decided that she would ask if she could borrow it so that some nights she could drive across and see her grandfather. It might not do any good, but at least it would ease her conscience.

When she came down to dinner, though, the pleasure left her face. They had a guest, and although Damon introduced them politely, telling her that it was Leonie Saddler, she did not really have to be told. This was the woman who had been watching with very spiteful eyes when Damon had made her look such a fool over the matter of the books.

Catherine had to pull herself together quickly. She had a great urge to glare. She felt as if the woman was an intruder, and that was ridiculous; if anyone was intruding it was herself. She was so settled here that she had not expected anyone else to arrive, and now that someone had she was startled to find that she resented it.

Not that Damon chatted endlessly to her at dinnertime in normal circumstances, and very frequently she took her lunch with Mrs Jarvis, but she had looked forward to these dinnertimes after she had got herself settled, and here was someone to break up the tranquillity of things.

'It's very unusual for us to be dining with a third party, darling,' Leonie said, smiling sweetly at Damon. Her voice, however, contained a certain amount of acid which Catherine did not miss.

Catherine had to admit that Miss Saddler looked lovely. Her hair was beautifully arranged and she was dressed perfectly. Catherine wore little make-up because her dark colouring was sufficient, but Leonie Saddler had the confidence that showed she knew how well she looked. She was perfectly at ease, and even after a week here Catherine was rarely that when Damon was near.

It seemed quite obvious to Catherine that Leonie was going to spend the evening doing her best to make things uncomfortable, and she steeled herself for it. She would eat her meal and then disappear, leaving them to get on with whatever it was they did in private. She composed her face and sat down at the table.

Later she decided it was the most unpleasant meal of her life. Leonie kept up a stream of conversation all the time, deliberately cutting Catherine out, not even bothering to be polite in any way at all. She was treating Catherine like a servant, and Damon seemed quite indifferent to it.

From time to time he addressed a few words to her, but she was sure it was from sheer politeness and not that he had any wish to speak to her. When their eyes met she found it very difficult not to look miserable, because she felt inexplicably lonely.

Leonie's dark red gown was obviously costly, and Catherine felt very much like a poor relation in her plain blue woollen dress. They stayed at the table for a long time too, because Leonie didn't want to move to the drawing-room for coffee, and Catherine became more and more uncomfortable. It left her sitting there with them, and she wanted to leave.

'We really must go into the other room now or Mrs Jarvis will never get finished,' Damon said finally after a close look at Catherine's strained face. He held Leonie's chair for her, but before he could do the same for Catherine she had sprung to her feet.

'I'll leave you alone,' she said, managing a little smile. 'I've got loads of things to do.' She turned quickly to the door, but Damon's voice stopped her.

'Don't go, Catherine,' he ordered softly, and she looked round with rising panic. She just didn't want to stay and see him with that woman, and the realisation was devastating. What was the matter with her? He was absolutely nothing to her at all. She didn't even like him. He was the enemy!

'I—I don't really want coffee,' she assured him desperately. 'If you'll excuse me...' She almost fled from

the room, but she didn't miss the final remark that
Leonie threw in her direction, deliberately designed for
her to hear.

'What a strange girl. She seems quite boring, darling.
Do you have to eat with her every night? She's only a
glorified secretary, after all.'

Catherine never heard Damon's reply. She ran upstairs, telling herself that Leonie Saddler was the sort of
woman he deserved. A woman like that fitted in with
his important, powerful world, a cold, hard woman. She
reminded herself that Damon was cold and hard too,
that he was cruelly keeping her here, but inside she was
upset and she knew it

In her room she spent quite a long time walking around
in agitation and then decided that she had better pack
a bag for tomorrow morning. She was not quite sure
how she was going to get home, but she could ring Robin
and ask him to come over and fetch her. She certainly
was not going to ask Damon if he would take her, and
before she came back here again she would have to have
her own transport. She would not be beholden to Damon
in any way.

But as she fumed it was not Damon's face that was
in her mind; it was Leonie Saddler's. The woman had
irritated her more than normal because, generally
speaking, Catherine laughed at people who annoyed her
and then put them from her mind. This time, though,
that face and the gleaming blonde hair that surrounded
it were lingering in her mind like a small bead of poison.
Her strong feelings frightened her because she had never
had them before.

She had actually showered and got ready for bed before
she remembered about her grandfather. So much for
thinking of other people! There was nothing for it but
to go down to her own office.

She looked out of the window, but Leonie's car was still there, and Catherine knew she would have to get down the stairs unseen. She certainly was not going to hang around until about two in the morning waiting. She put on her dressing-gown, tightened the sash around her slender waist, and cautiously opened the door to make her way along the passage upstairs.

At the top of the stairs she paused. She would not like to be caught in her night attire as Leonie Saddler stood in her beautiful gown and made nasty comments. She couldn't even hear voices, though, so she went quickly downstairs, across the hall and into her own office, closing the door quietly behind her, greatly relieved that she had made it to base.

Catherine made the call to her grandfather very quick indeed, because she wanted to get back upstairs before anyone came out. He was quite cheerful, although he sounded very tired.

'Shall we be seeing you tomorrow?' he asked.

'Certainly,' Catherine assured him. 'He's not said anything about it, but if he thinks he's keeping me here all over the weekend he's greatly mistaken!'

'That's my girl.' Her grandfather laughed. 'You show him.'

Catherine nodded to herself. She would if it became necessary. Speaking to her grandfather cheered her up— it always did. Whatever happened to Gramps, she knew he would battle to the last, and she had the same sort of spirit herself.

She quietly replaced the phone and switched off the light in the study, and it was at that moment that the drawing-room door opened and she heard voices in the hall. Just a few minutes more and she would have been upstairs. Now she would have to wait here, standing around in the dark, almost as if she was hiding.

She peeped carefully through the window. They had not even made it to the car yet, and she felt very cross, not particularly because they were wasting her time—she had nothing special to do with it—but because she hated to be put into a situation where she felt guilty. Now, for some absurd reason, she felt like a burglar who had come in to use the telephone and been caught at it.

They were not going to catch her at it, though; she was sure of that. She heard the front door open and decided to give them a few minutes to say goodnight. When Damon came in she would listen for his footsteps and make a dash upstairs. She heard the front door close and waited quietly, but it seemed ages before a car pulled away.

Catherine heard Damon's footsteps coming across the hall and breathed a sigh of relief. Soon he would be going up the stairs or into his study and she could get back up to her own room. She heard him go to his study door, but to her great surprise she heard it being locked. She could understand that really, though. He must have a lot of confidential papers in there. She heard him come back across the hall, surprised to find that she now knew his footsteps. It was amazing how quickly she had got to know little things about him. She was pondering on that when a key was inserted into her own office door and turned very firmly.

For a few seconds she just couldn't believe it. Why was he locking her door too? Did he go round at night locking every door in the house? Astonishment kept her still for quite a few minutes, and then she realised that she was locked in. He had already walked away, and as far as she knew he was already going upstairs. She had been too surprised to listen.

Catherine sprang forward to the door and rattled at the knob. It did no good whatsoever—he really had locked it. She banged on the door very loudly, and when nothing happened she banged again and shouted. She was still banging when the door was unlocked and pushed open, and Damon stood in the lighted hallway, looking into the darkness at her.

'What the hell are you doing?' he rasped.

'You locked me in.' He was standing there making her feel as if she'd been up to something criminal, and she felt guilty for no good reason. It annoyed her, and she snapped, 'You know perfectly well why I'm here.'

'I never know why you do things,' he grated. 'You seem to live in another world entirely, with rules you've just made up. This, however, is in my own house and I would very much like to know what you're doing in here, in the darkness.' He switched on the lights, and Catherine blinked in the sudden brilliance. 'Undressed,' he added quietly, his dark brows raised.

Catherine's face was bright with embarrassment, and the desire to fight back began to ebb away.

'You know I come down every night to phone my grandfather. It was your own suggestion,' she pointed out quietly.

'Normally you phone immediately after dinner.' He still stood there watching her coldly, and she almost choked.

'You check up on me?'

'Not particularly,' he assured her acidly. 'I vaguely know that you come into the study after dinner. Tonight was different, was it?'

'You had a guest,' she reminded him miserably. He knew just how different tonight had been.

'Leonie would not in any way have wished to come and hear your conversation,' he murmured drily.

Catherine looked past him, wanting to run into the hall and escape, but he was standing in her way.

'We lingered longer than usual and I didn't get around to phoning Grandfather. I was ready for bed and then I realised I hadn't phoned him.'

'It seems a reasonable excuse.' He was looking at her as if he was pondering the matter and deciding whether to let her off or not, and Catherine began to get annoyed.

'I don't *need* an excuse! It was your idea that I use this telephone. I just happened to forget to phone him earlier because tonight was unusual.'

'I frequently have guests for dinner. Leonie often comes.'

'It's the first time you've had a guest since I've been here,' Catherine muttered, realising that all this was most unfortunate. He was back to hard suspicion, and being in a darkened study, standing quietly instead of coming out boldly and going upstairs, was really a very suspicious thing to do. 'I can understand why you locked me in, but now you've let me out. Thank you very much.'

She made to pass him, but his hand came out and grasped her arm, his fingers strong through the thin material of her dressing-gown.

'One moment,' he said coldly. 'What were you doing *besides* phoning your grandfather?'

'Nothing.' She looked up at him in surprise and found that she was being assessed in a narrow-eyed way, the icy look back on his face. 'How was I to know you were going to go round locking all doors as if this were a prison?'

'I always lock my study door at night. There are a lot of things in there I wouldn't like other people to see, and as you're working with me I lock your door too.'

'*I* didn't know that,' Catherine said huffily.

'Of course you didn't. It's unlocked before you come down in the morning.' He was still staring at her, trying to get into her mind, and she could have screamed with frustration. At the moment there was nothing in there but a vague sort of distress. He could save himself the trouble. There was certainly nothing for her to feel guilty about, although she did feel all manner of a fool.

'Well, if the episode is over I'll go to bed,' she said tightly.

'You do that, Miss Farrell.'

He was back to calling her Miss Farrell, and it hadn't taken him long to regress—he had been calling her Catherine all week. Now it seemed that nothing had changed at all.

She was just moving when he said, 'Why were you standing in the dark? Why didn't you simply come out and go to bed?'

'I—I was undressed ...'

'You still are.'

'Yes, but I didn't mean ... I didn't want anybody to see me and——'

'I can see you now, and I've been looking at you for much longer than I would have been if you had simply rushed out and fled up the stairs. Or was it Leonie who worried you?'

'Nobody worried me, Mr King,' Catherine assured him breathlessly. She was desperate to rush off and be out of his sight, but he was deliberately keeping her here. It was the same sort of cruel deliberation he had used when he had let her bump into him.

'Then why did you desert me after dinner so rapidly?'

'I—I had things to do. I had to pack.' Catherine felt he was tying her in knots, and she was getting more anxious by the second.

'To pack? Should I know about this latest plan?'

'When I go home tomorrow——' she began un-happily, hearing the mockery that was certainly edged with cruelty.

'Oh, you're going home, are you?' he murmured darkly, and Catherine turned round to look up at him, expecting him to forbid it now.

'But why not? Surely you don't intend to keep me here all weekend?'

'I'm not actually *keeping* you here. You're working here—it's slightly different,' he pointed out smoothly, and Catherine blushed more deeply. He was getting the most out of this situation, and she was powerless to stop him. She started again.

'You don't expect me to work all weekend, do you?'

'On this occasion, no. Nothing much is happening. Of course, I go overseas quite a lot, and when I do I'll expect you to be here all the time.'

'Very well,' Catherine said quietly. 'I can well understand that, Mr King.'

She turned away, upset and embarrassed, but as she turned a big moth flew close to her, and she jumped with alarm as it swooped on her, its wings brushing her face. Moths were one thing she just didn't like, and she gave a small shriek, covering her head with her hands and backing away.

She backed right into Damon and his hands came to her shoulders, his fingers probing the slender bones. He began to laugh, his cold annoyance going very swiftly, and his voice softened to dark humour.

'Will you stop it, Catherine?' His eyes were filled with amusement as he turned her round. 'It's a moth, not a pterodactyl.'

'You must have let it in,' she muttered, glancing anxiously behind her, and worried by the fact that he was holding her again.

'Deliberately,' he mocked. 'I knew you were hiding and I thought a moth might just be punishment enough for deserting me after dinner.' He turned her face back and looked down at her. 'I doubt if moths bite people.

In any case, I wouldn't let it bite you.' He smiled into her eyes. 'All right, I've stopped being annoyed. You're valuable as a source of amusement if nothing else. Are we going to be at each other's throats all the time?'

'We're not at each other's throats all the time,' Catherine pointed out, carefully detaching herself from his grasp. The moth was now settled on the front door and things looked safer, but not if she stayed firmly under his hands. 'I'm here to work for you, Mr King, and that's all, and if I'm not really valuable then dismiss me.'

'Certainly not, Miss Farrell,' he taunted, his lips twisting wryly. 'I have plans.'

'I know,' Catherine said bitterly. 'I also know you're suspicious of me.'

'Can you blame me? You're surely a suspicious character. Tonight was a perfect example.'

'I'm glad it amused you,' Catherine snapped as she spun round and set off upstairs, determined to escape, but she didn't quite manage it.

'How do you intend to get home tomorrow?' he asked softly.

'I'll ask Robin to call for me.' She didn't even bother to look round, and Damon's answer quite shocked her.

'I'm going into London. If you're ready about nine I'll take you and drop you off at your house.'

She turned round and stared at him in surprise. 'I couldn't possibly put you to that trouble.'

'What trouble?' He shrugged easily. 'I'm going into town. I'll take you with me. After all, I brought you here. Do you want me to collect you on Monday morning?'

'No!' Catherine said quickly. 'Robin has a car. I—I'm going to borrow it, if he'll let me. You don't have to do this.'

'Oh, I know.'

She realised that he was laughing at her again, his amber eyes dancing with amusement, and she quickly ran through the things she had said. As far as she could see there was nothing at all to laugh at in any of this, unless he was comparing her with Leonie. He had come straight from seeing that beautiful gown to seeing her in her rather worn dressing-gown.

She said goodnight in a small voice and walked off upstairs with as much dignity as she could muster, well aware that his eyes were following her all the time. She didn't know what he was thinking, but it was sure to be to her disadvantage.

The whole episode had shaken her, and it took a long time to go to sleep. She heard Damon come along to his room, and her mind turned over what it would be like inside his room. What sort of furniture did he have? Did he like very plain things, or was it a beautiful room like hers? She very much doubted that fact. As she fell asleep she was wondering how many times Leonie Saddler had been in that room.

In the morning Damon took her home. It was a pleasant drive on a lovely spring day, and the powerful car got them quickly into London. Catherine offered to get off and go by Tube, but he insisted on taking her right to the house.

She was quite sure he would find it all very much below his dignity, but to her surprise he seemed to be quite at home in the area. Of course, the house her grandfather owned would have fitted several times into Ravenhall Manor, and she half expected someone like Damon to turn his nose up at the place, but he did not. He sat for a minute looking at the house with an odd kind of pleasure on his face that puzzled her.

'Thank you,' Catherine said quietly. 'It's very kind of you.'

'I'm not really kind,' he assured her. 'In any case, this is part of the perks of the job.'

'You won't need to do it any more,' she told him quickly. 'I'm sure Robin will lend me his car.'

'We'll see.'

He drove off, and Catherine breathed a sigh of relief. Home at last. The week had been something of a strain, but now she could be herself. She was beginning to wonder who herself was. Damon seemed to have made her feel permanently uneasy and foolish.

Gramps seemed all right. He greeted her very enthusiastically. Robin was out, and she was a little bit miffed at that. One would have thought that he could stay in on Saturday morning until she arrived to look after her grandfather, but he had not. She set to immediately, and by lunchtime the whole place was spick and span and her grandfather was settled in his chair watching television. It was easy just to slide back into her old ways, and in the afternoon she went shopping.

She had to go right into the city, and she was surprised to hear her name called.

'Miss Farrell!'

It was Gordon Turner, and he was swinging along towards her with a smile on his face, obviously pleased to see her. It was nice to be looked at as if she was normal and not some crook. There was nothing at all worrying about Gordon Turner, and Catherine smiled back at him.

'Fancy seeing you,' he said, coming up to her. 'Where are you going?'

'Just shopping. It's a normal weekend chore.'

'So you've escaped from the haunted manor?' he asked, laughing down at her.

'Is it haunted?' Catherine wanted to know, very interested at once.

'God knows! But I would imagine any ghost who appeared would quickly disappear at the sight of our Mr King.'

Catherine smiled, but she felt she should not be talking about Damon. Over the weeks she had begun to feel differently about him, and she found to her astonishment that she resented other people saying anything about him at all.

She remembered last night and how he had laughed about her fear of moths. She remembered looking back down as she had finally got to the top of the stairs. He had still been watching her, a slight smile on his face. It had given her a strange feeling that she had not even shaken off this morning.

She went for coffee with Gordon, and when they came back out on to the sunny streets he said, 'I've got two tickets for a concert tonight; I don't suppose you'd like to come?'

Catherine's immediate reaction was to say no. Not that she didn't want to go—it would be rather nice to go out for the evening—but she was sure that Robin would not be staying in, and she hadn't seen her grandfather all week. He must get quite lonely by himself.

'I don't think I can,' she said regretfully.

'Surely I'm not *that* off-putting?' Gordon asked wryly, and Catherine shook her head.

'It isn't that. There's my grandfather. I've been away all week and I feel I ought to be with him over the weekend.'

'Well, I can't offer to take him too. I've only got two tickets.'

'It was good of you to ask me,' Catherine assured him seriously.

'How about dinner, then? That won't take long.'

She hesitated even so. 'Can I ring you? I'll just see what's happening at home. My brother might be staying in.'

'Robin?' Gordon suddenly asked. 'He works with the firm, doesn't he?'

'Yes, I'm surprised you know. He's a very small cog in the wheel of things.'

'Oh, I know most people. After all, I deal with most of their salaries,' he pointed out drily.

Catherine promised to ring him and went home quite pleased with herself. Her life was taking a turn for the better. Obviously Gordon didn't think she was boring, no matter what Leonie Saddler's opinion was.

Her grandfather wouldn't hear of her staying in, and he was quite sure that one of these days Robin would stay in at night. Robin came in just then, and Catherine thought it best not to pounce on him suddenly. She would have a quiet word with him in the morning about where he went at night and ask him if he could sometimes stay in with her grandfather while she was away. After all, she was not going to be working at Damon King's house forever.

She did mention about the car, though. She thought she would get that over quickly, but to her annoyance Robin was not too pleased.

'I can't lend you my car, Cath,' he told her firmly. 'You know perfectly well I have to use it at night.'

'Have you ever thought about staying in at night?' she asked, deciding to take both matters on at once.

'Whatever for?' He looked at her as if she were mad, and it made Catherine more annoyed than ever.

'For Gramps! I'm accustomed to being in with him, but you could do your bit,' she pointed out, keeping her voice low. They were standing in the kitchen, and she certainly didn't want her grandfather to be involved in this. 'I'll only be away working at Ravenhall for a short time. I would have thought you could stay in with him once or twice.'

'He's all right! He's got television and his books. He's not ill in bed or anything like that,' Robin said stroppily.

'No, he isn't, but it would be nice for him to have someone to talk to if I'm going to be away for any length of time, and you're never at home. He's going to forget how to talk.'

'Not him,' Robin muttered. 'Gramps would never forget how to talk. He's been talking fifty to the dozen for as long as I can remember.'

They had to agree to leave it, but Catherine would not let the matter of the car go.

'Look, if you can't lend me your car, then I'm going to have to rely on Damon King to fetch me back and forth.'

'I can't, Cath, and that's all there is to it. I've got things to do. Apart from going to the gigs and apart from the jobs I've got at the clubs, I've got—well—things.'

'You're really selfish,' Catherine snapped, glaring at him.

'It's not selfishness; you know I'd never be selfish with you,' he protested. 'It's just that one or two things are happening at the moment and I've got to have transport.'

'Oh, fine,' Catherine seethed. 'That means I've got to ring up Damon King like a fool and ask him to take me back on Monday morning.'

'Oh, I can do that, but it will have to be Sunday night,' Robin said brightly.

Catherine glared at him.

'You mean I've got to go back to Ravenhall on Sunday night because you can't get up a bit earlier on Monday morning to take me?'

After a few further words of argument he agreed. On Monday morning he would take her, but she could not keep the car, and Catherine had to be content with that. He also rather grudgingly offered to stay in that night, pointing out that it was Saturday and a big club night and that this was a very great sacrifice to make.

Catherine let him make it. Normally she would have given in, but she was feeling rather annoyed with Robin. She felt that there was a streak of selfishness in him that she had not seen before. She rang up Gordon and agreed to go out with him, not for the whole evening, but for dinner. It seemed to be necessary to establish her rights. She had been looking after Robin as well as Gramps for a long time now, and Robin had slipped into an acceptance of it.

Catherine enjoyed the evening. Gordon was very easy to get on with and set about entertaining her right from the first. He was an amusing man. He was not at all threatening in any way, and she was able to relax with him. She was quite startled to find that she was comparing him with Damon, quite startled to find too that she found certain things about him that were sadly lacking as far as comparison with her boss was concerned.

He had not got the same hard, handsome features. There was a softness about him that might have been kindliness but might perhaps have been lack of the strength of character that Damon possessed. She always thought of Damon as being born with a silver spoon in his mouth, but when she thought carefully about his face she wondered about that. Somewhere along the line he had been through a hard time. It was sheer instinct and probably not true, but she just felt it.

'Daydreaming?' Gordon asked.

'No. As a matter of fact...' Catherine jumped guiltily '...I was thinking about the boss.'

'Got you scared, has he?'

'He did at first, but not now.'

'What's it like at that house?' Gordon wanted to know, and instantly Catherine found herself closing up. It was not so much anything to do with confidentiality or loyalty, it was a feeling of protectiveness, and that quite startled her.

'Oh, beautiful,' she said. 'Of course, I'm only the working girl. I hardly get out of my own office.'

Gordon looked at her steadily for a minute and nodded.

'I can see you've settled into Judith Greaves' ways very quickly,' he said quietly. 'She wouldn't talk about him either.'

'There's nothing to talk about,' Catherine said quickly. 'He's not a man that you really get to know.'

'No.' Gordon shook his head, staring at her and trying to see what she was thinking. There was not much chance of that. Damon had tried it and he had not succeeded; at least she didn't think he had. All the same, she was careful what she said from then on. She seemed to be moving in exalted circles, but she was not about to let it go to her head. She had to be loyal. Catherine was very quiet when she realised it was a little more than loyalty. It was Damon. He certainly didn't need her protection, but it seemed to be almost instinctive to shield him.

CHAPTER FIVE

ON MONDAY morning Robin drove Catherine down to Ravenhall, but he was obviously unwilling and edgy.

'You'll be in plenty of time for work,' she assured him as they sped down the motorway.

'I wanted to be early this morning. This is creating a bit of a problem.'

'I could have walked, of course,' Catherine murmured, and Robin shot her an apologetic look.

'Oh, Cath, don't! It's just that things are happening...'

She didn't press the matter. He was becoming secretive, almost another person. At one time he would have blurted his worries out to her, but he never did that now. Their rapport seemed to have gone. It had been slowly going over the past few months, and prying would be useless.

It was with a great reluctance that he drove her up to the house, and she was quite sure that he would have preferred to dump her at the gate with her bag. That was startling too. Not long ago he had been wanting Damon to notice him, but now it seemed he wanted to be as far away as possible.

They went up the curving drive at some speed, and before Catherine had time to catch her breath her bag was on the step, Robin was back in the car, and the bright red Ford was tearing down the drive.

She was still looking after him with a startled expression on her face when Damon came to the door.

'That was quick.' His narrowed eyes followed the car. 'I take it you couldn't borrow the car after all.'

'He needed it,' Catherine said quickly, very well used to making excuses for Robin. 'Still, it doesn't matter; he got me here.'

'Very quickly by the look of it.' Damon frowned after the car. 'I could have got you here with a great deal more safety. I'm not sure that car is fit to be on the road.'

'It manages.' Catherine suddenly looked up and smiled brilliantly, realising that she was very happy to be back here. She acknowledged too that she had missed Damon. She was quite accustomed to looking up and seeing him now, quite accustomed to hearing his footsteps around the house. His very presence had become familiar to her, and she missed him when he was not at home. There was no air of menace about him this morning, and he stared down at her for a moment.

'You're happy to be back,' he pronounced softly, and Catherine quickly pulled herself together.

'I'm a workaholic.'

He gave her a wry look and picked up her bag. 'Then let's get started.'

She was back at work, ready to start, brisk and efficient, but inside her mind was telling her that in actual fact she was just happy. It was very foolish and something she would really have to watch out for. She was not on holiday, she was in a situation that was dictated entirely by a man who would have no qualms about causing a great deal of trouble if the need arose, but it was very easy to forget that.

During the morning she was very busy, and just before lunch she looked up to find Damon watching her from the doorway, his eyes faintly sardonic.

'Making yourself indispensable?'

'Of course,' she said pertly. 'I don't want to lose my job, do I?'

'Not much chance of that.' He came in and put some papers on her desk. 'I'm leaving now. I'll be out for most of the afternoon. I've got a meeting in town, and some time this week I'll have to fly over to Japan.'

She was surprised at the feeling of dismay it gave her, and she just looked at him blankly.

'Oh, you'll be away.'

'I can't see any method of getting to Japan without leaving the house,' Damon mused wryly, and Catherine flushed with confusion.

'It—it's just that I hadn't expected it.'

'You'll manage,' he said briskly, turning to the door. 'You're doing very well, as a matter of fact.'

'Am I?' Catherine spoke very quietly, and he spun round to look at her.

'Believe me, I wouldn't have said it if you were not.' He held her gaze lingeringly, and she felt very vulnerable with those golden eyes on her.

'How long will you be away?' Catherine used her most efficient voice, and it seemed to snap him to the present.

'I've no idea—a couple of days. I'll be in touch with you.'

'You mean you'll phone me from Japan?' She sounded a little awestricken, and Damon smiled his strange crooked smile.

'We really can afford the bill. It's no big deal. I'll want to know what's been happening.' He turned to leave and then turned round again. 'Did you have a nice weekend?'

It made Catherine wonder what sort of a weekend he had had, and she knew he had probably been out with Leonie, going to some glamorous place, living a life she knew nothing of.

'I went out to dinner.' She had an urgent wish to be interesting, not to be someone who could be dismissed as boring.

'That's nice.' He was looking amused again, and she wanted to impress on him that she had been to a glamorous place too.

'I went out with Gordon Turner,' she informed him brightly, but his reaction startled her. The smile died out of his eyes at once.

'My chief accountant?'

'Yes. I met him while I was working with Judith. He asked me out for the evening.'

'So that's why you were so anxious to have the weekend off. I assumed you were worried about your grandfather. How foolish of me.'

He turned and walked out, leaving her stunned. Until she had mentioned Gordon he had been almost indulgent. Now he was furious. Once again, too, he had assumed that her motives were selfish. The guilty feeling about leaving her grandfather for even one evening was back with some force, and her happy feeling of belonging had gone.

She looked out of the window as the door slammed, and Damon was going down the front steps, his face like thunder. What had she done—gone out with one of his higher-ranking slaves? Had she stepped above her station in the order of things?

When he came back from the meeting it was late, and at dinner he was stiffly formal. Catherine assumed he was still annoyed about earlier, and she was quite miserable.

'Will you be going to Japan straight away?' she asked when the silence became impossible.

'No.' He looked across at her coldly, none of the mockery about him that had grown since she had met him. 'I'm not going at all. I think it would be very wise to stay here for the present.'

'I thought I was managing well?' Catherine looked at him in surprise, but if anything his face tightened further.

'You are,' he said shortly. 'Perhaps too well. Something is sure to go wrong when things are running smoothly. It would be wise for me to be around.'

His voice was edged with ice, and Catherine had no idea what he meant. It was obvious that something today had infuriated him, and she could only assume that it was her.

When she phoned home her grandfather sounded more tired than ever. It left her very worried, and she knew this could not continue. It was her duty and her responsibility to be at home. If Damon wanted to get rid of her, and Robin too, then he would just have to do it. She decided to tell him in the morning that she would have to give up this job if she had to continue working from Ravenhall. Gramps came first. Better to be without money than to have him ill and alone.

Catherine was awakened by someone banging on the door, and before she had time to do more than get the light on Mrs Jarvis came into the room. She was in her dressing-gown, and Catherine was surprised to see as she glanced at the clock that it was two in the morning.

'You've got to get up straight away, Catherine,' the housekeeper said urgently. 'There's been a phone call from your brother. I took it because Mr King switches his phone off at night and I heard the phone in the hall ringing.'

Catherine sat up in bed, still dazed from sleep, and the housekeeper looked at her worriedly.

'It's your grandfather, dear. I think you'd better come at once.'

Catherine sprang out of bed, and for those few seconds she didn't know what to do. All her worst fears were realised. Something was happening to Gramps and she wasn't there.

She made a dive for the door, but even as she did she realised that she was stuck out here with no way of getting back. Robin had not given her the car after all. At least he had been there, unless he had been out and then come back in to find Gramps collapsed. She didn't know what to do.

Mrs Jarvis bustled downstairs, muttering about making some tea, but Catherine didn't want tea, she only wanted to get to her grandfather, and there was only one person to get her there. She rushed along the passage, and didn't have any trouble finding Damon, because one of the doors had a light underneath it.

She almost fell on the door, hammering away, and before he had even answered she opened the door and rushed inside, oblivious to everything except the fact that her grandfather was ill.

'Catherine?' He was sitting up in bed, obviously having just been awakened, but for a few seconds she didn't really see him. Her eyes were wide with fright and she just stared at him, until it suddenly dawned on her that he was wearing no pyjama jacket and that she had put herself into a very awkward situation by rushing in here. Even so, she couldn't stop.

'Oh, please, you've got to help me!' she begged. 'It's my grandfather! Mrs Jarvis just woke me up because Robin phoned. Gramps is ill.'

'Get dressed,' Damon said quickly. 'I'll take you home.'

She nodded, too numb to move, and Damon eyed her sternly.

'Catherine!' He spoke sharply, and she pulled herself together.

'I—I'm sorry. I just rushed in here and——'

'It's all right. Just go and get dressed. We'll be on our way as quickly as possible.'

She realised then that she had not even bothered to put a dressing-gown on. She was standing there in a silky nightie, the straps falling over her shoulders, her hair all tousled around her, and his eyes were running over her in the way they usually did. Her cheeks flushed when she realised that she had probably embarrassed him a great deal.

'Hurry up, Catherine,' he said very calmly, and she just nodded and rushed out.

As she came from her room, Damon was coming out of his, dressed ready for a trip through the night to London. They got to the top of the stairs at the same time, and Mrs Jarvis was just coming up. She had a tray of tea, but Damon looked at Catherine's white face and waved it aside.

'I don't think she could drink it, Mrs Jarvis.'

'I'm sorry,' Catherine said, looking into the sympathetic face of the older woman. 'I've got to get home as quickly as possible.'

'He's not at home, dear. Your brother said he'd managed to get him to hospital. You're to go straight there.'

Catherine's face went whiter still, and Damon took her arm, hurrying her down the steps and out to the car. Inside she was cold and numb. She had expected this, had been expecting it for weeks, but now that it was here she was not in any way prepared. It had been a dark cloud at the back of her mind for some considerable time.

Damon glanced at her and then looked away, setting the car in motion. She looked dazed, and he had never seen anyone with such a white face before. Her eyes looked enormous, staring out into the blackness, following the headlights of the car.

'He has a bad heart.' The sound of her voice after a long time had him glancing at her again, taking his eyes momentarily from the road. 'I knew something was going to happen when I was away. I was going to tell you in the morning that I wanted to go back, that I wanted to give the job up if I had to stay at Ravenhall. I should have done it before. If only I'd been there.'

'Don't torture yourself, Catherine,' he commanded. 'In all probability there would have been nothing you could have done even if you had been there. At least your brother was there and he's got him to hospital. You couldn't have done more than that.'

'I could have watched him more. Sometimes Robin is selfish.' She shook her head impatiently. 'I shouldn't be saying that. I shouldn't be blaming Robin. I should have been watching Gramps myself.'

'He's had a heart attack,' Damon said quietly. 'That's what your brother told Mrs Jarvis. Watching wouldn't have stopped that.'

'I know. I'm just hoping, really, hanging on to slender threads.'

She was silent again, and he cast a slanting look at her. She had drawn in on herself and was holding herself tightly together. Her black hair was flowing around her white face as she stared ahead. He put on as much speed as he could, but he suspected that they would be too late, and he thought she knew too.

In the bright lights of the hospital she hurried forward as they saw Robin sitting outside a room, his head in his hands.

'It's no use, Cath.' Robin stood as she came to him. 'He died a minute ago. You were just too late to see him. Give yourself a few seconds and then go in.'

He reached for her, but she stepped away. Every one of her muscles was tense, and she didn't want him to hold her; she just wanted to see her grandfather and say goodbye. Her eyes were quite empty, and Damon looked at her steadily before she turned and walked into the room. There was something in the topaz gaze that gave her courage, and she needed it. Gramps was gone from her life.

When she came out again Damon was walking about outside the room, and he turned round at the sound of her footsteps.

'I'll take Catherine home,' he offered, and Robin nodded his thanks.

'There are one or two things to do. I'll have to stay here.'

'I'll stay here with you,' Catherine murmured dully, but Robin shook his head.

'It's just formalities. I'd rather you were at home, Cath. I don't think I'll be too long.'

She just turned away, hardly aware of it when Damon took her arm and steered her very carefully towards the door. He didn't say anything. He just drove through the early morning traffic and finally parked in the darkness outside the house.

When she made no move to get out he turned to look at her and saw tears streaming absolutely silently down her face. She had felt them coming, forcing their way into her eyes, hot moisture that seemed to burn her eyelids. She had not cried for a long time, but now she had no control whatever over her feelings.

She tried to blink away the tears, but they moved further down her cheeks. She could feel their progress but could do nothing to stop them, and she was completely unresisting when Damon reached across and collected her.

'Come here,' he said softly. 'It's all right, Catherine. Cry. It's the best thing for you.'

He pulled her to his shoulder and she came willingly, her silky hair against his neck, and his hands stroked through it soothingly. His very presence was a comfort, and she just let the tears fall. There was nothing she

could do, and somehow, with Damon's arms around her,
she calmed. Even if she had been there on time, she could
not have brought about any miracle.

She cried quietly, and Damon just let her until the
tears stopped and just misery remained. Then he cupped
her face in his hands and took out a white handkerchief
to wipe her cheeks. She was trembling, and the hands
that came to finish the job for herself were cold and
shaking.

'I'm not leaving you alone,' he said quietly. 'I'm
coming in with you.' His voice was firm and cool, and
she nodded, searching in her bag for the key. She didn't
want him to go. She felt lonely.

As Catherine switched on the lights the shock of the
small house hit her hard. Her grandfather seemed to be
everywhere, but she didn't cry again. She walked away
into the kitchen, holding herself stiffly, not aware that
Damon followed.

'I'll make some tea.' It was even difficult to recognise
her own voice, and Damon looked at her sharply.

'I'll do it. I haven't forgotten how to make tea.' He
was right behind her, but she felt now that she was im-
posing on him, and she fought to control herself.

'I'm all right,' she assured him in a brittle voice. 'I
can manage very well.'

'I know. I'll just hang around all the same.' His eyes
met hers, and she had no idea how tragic she looked at
that moment, how the tears still clung to her long lashes.
Damon turned away from her abruptly and asked in a
harsh voice, 'Where are the cups?'

'They're in the cupboard, but I'll get them.' She
quickly sensed his change of mood and was instantly
agitated. 'You don't really have to stay, you know, if
you want to go... I don't need——'

'Damn it all, Catherine,' he grated, swinging round
to scowl at her. 'What do you think I am, some sort of

monster?' She just stared up at him, and he turned away
impatiently. 'Yes, you probably do,' he muttered. 'I'm
trying to help, trying to make myself useful. The only
other thing I can think of doing is holding you close to
make things all right. We've already done that, so let's
get the tea, shall we?'

His words startled her out of her misery, and she gazed
at him for a moment as he began to reach for the cups.
She wanted him to hold her until she felt better, but at
this moment it seemed that it would take a very long
time. She couldn't think of anyone else who could make
her better, though. It had to be Damon.

Catherine had a week off work. There were lots of things
that had to be seen to, and she felt that it was all down
to her. Whatever had to be faced, she would be the one
who had to face it, because Robin seemed to have gone
all to pieces. When he had come back from the hospital
Damon had still been there, refusing to leave until
Catherine had someone with her. He had been his usual
polite self with her brother, but she'd noticed that he
watched Robin very carefully, trying to make his mind
up.

In spite of his kindness and in spite of the fact that
he was there when she needed him, Damon still suspected both of them. The fact that she had been at his
house hadn't made one bit of difference.

Damon gave Robin a week off too, and Catherine
thought later it would have been better if Robin had gone
to work. He did nothing but roam around the house,
and a lot of the time he simply seemed to be staring into
space. He never made a move to go out at night and
leave her, but sometimes she wished he would, because
their conversation seemed to have dwindled down to nil.

The worst time was the funeral. Catherine had never
felt so lonely before. There was a drizzly rain, and every-

thing seemed quite out of keeping with the happy,
forceful person her grandfather had been. Robin just
stood with his head bowed in the rain, unable to help
himself, let alone her, and she found her mind searching
for Damon, wishing he were there, missing him badly.

Towards the end of the week Robin seemed to pull
himself together and announced one evening that he was
going out. He didn't come in until the very early hours
of the morning, and it set a pattern, because even though
he was not at work he was out again next day.

On Friday Catherine realised that she didn't even feel
like going out shopping. She was at home by herself.
She cleaned the house automatically because it had to
be done, and then she walked out into the garden. Her
interest in that had gone too, because it was her grandfather's garden, something they had always done
together. It was a cold day, but she never thought to
move indoors, even though she was shivering. She just
stood there, not really seeing anything at all.

She didn't hear Damon arrive. He came round the
back, and at the sound of his footsteps she looked up,
tears on her face. She was surprised to see him, but he
looked very angry.

'Are you trying to get pneumonia?' He came across
to her and took her inside at once. 'It's bitterly cold out
there.'

'I was looking at things,' she explained miserably, hurt
by the harsh sound of his voice.

'And drowning in misery. It's time to stop all that. I
want you back.' He hustled her into the sitting-room,
and she turned round to look at him.

'But it's not a week!'

'It's long enough.' He still looked angry, and she
couldn't cope with it.

'I've got to stay here,' she protested. 'It's like
treachery, going away so soon, as if my grandfather had

never existed. You can dismiss me if you want, but——'

'It's over, Catherine,' he interrupted harshly. 'All you're hanging on to now is misery. You've got to start living again, and I *need* you!'

'Do you only ever think about yourself?' Catherine burst out bitterly, and his eyes narrowed at her tone.

'More often than not,' he informed her coldly. 'Where's your brother?' he added, and it worried her at once.

'He's out.' She automatically covered for Robin as usual. 'There were things to do.'

'I can imagine. It's time he was back at work too,' Damon said icily. He glanced round the neat and shining room. 'You've polished everything to a gloss. You've looked at the garden. I can't think there's much more for you to do here. The sooner you get back on with your life, the better.'

Catherine knew he was right, but at that moment she had an urgent desire to fight him. She wanted comfort, kindness, and all she was getting was a sort of controlled savagery. Their eyes clashed as she looked up at him angrily, but Damon was not giving any ground, and finally Catherine looked away.

'I'm sorry,' she said quietly. 'You're quite right, of course. However long I hang around here Gramps won't come back.'

'Stop that,' Damon said sharply. 'Accept things as they are, because things are not going to be different.'

'Is that what you do—accept things as they are because they're not going to be any different?' she asked, her grey eyes searching his face.

'I've never had any other choice; who does?' He turned away impatiently. 'I think we should wait until your brother comes in,' he added, and that worried Catherine a lot.

She had no idea where Robin was today, and she knew perfectly well that if he did not have things to do at home he should be back at work. Damon knew it too. She could see it in the cold amber eyes.

'I'll leave him a note.' She said it quickly, and Damon heard the anxiety in her voice.

'It might be the safest thing to do,' he murmured. 'It wouldn't be a good idea to clash with your brother at this time.'

'Why don't you just sack him if he irritates you so much?' she suggested bitterly, and Damon's hand shot out unexpectedly, tilting her face up.

'Why not indeed? I've never been lenient before in my life.' He looked into her eyes. 'And you? Do I get rid of you too, Catherine?'

'If—if you want to.' She tried to look away, but he tightened his grip, forcing her to meet his gaze.

'The chances of my letting you go are nil,' he muttered, turning away. 'I need you around, so don't go organising any great escape.'

It wasn't necessary to leave a note, because Robin came in at that moment. They heard his little red Ford draw up behind Damon's car, and Catherine went to the door to let him in. She wanted to warn him, and she looked at him, shaking her head, trying to signal to him that everything was all right. It wasn't a good idea, because Damon was standing in the hall behind her and he had not missed this little exchange.

Once again his face was hard with suspicion, and she could have wept. How could a man who had been so kind to her when she really needed him, who sometimes laughed and was quite indulgent, be as hard as he looked now, because of some stupid suspicion that anyone could have told him was ridiculous?

He didn't look at her; instead he spoke to Robin.

'Catherine is leaving. It's time she was back at work. She'll recover a lot more quickly at Ravenhall than she will here, surrounded by the past.'

For a second Robin appeared to be about to protest, but in face of Damon's cold power he said nothing. He just nodded and then moved to go past. It was quite obvious he was going up to his room to hide there, and Catherine felt very impatient with him. Damon was not about to let that happen.

'It's Friday,' he said firmly. 'On Monday I expect to see you back at work too.'

Robin spun round.

'I would have been, in any case!' He was quite truculent, daring in view of Damon's annoyance. 'I thought Cath was having until Monday off too.'

'She was, and I assure you she will not be overworked over the weekend, but now that she doesn't have to come home to see to her grandfather, now that she seems to have spent the week cleaning the house up and tidying the garden, I'm sure she'll be a lot more comfortable with my housekeeper to look after her and the tranquillity of my home around her.'

It was all rather possessive, and Catherine felt her face growing quite hot. Robin shot a startled look at her and then shrugged his shoulders and went upstairs. He was not being very nice and obviously wanted to get out of Damon's way as soon as possible, even pushing away politeness in order to escape. Damon certainly did not deserve this, and it made her feel very embarrassed.

Damon took it all in his stride however. He glanced at his watch.

'I've got one or two things to do in town. I'll be back for you in two hours; do you think you can be ready?'

Catherine just nodded, too disturbed to look at him, and he made quite an impatient sound and then went out. As soon as she saw his car pull away Catherine raced upstairs to speak to Robin.

'Did you have to be like that when we had a visitor?' she asked angrily. It was the first time she had felt in any sort of a temper since Gramps had died, and Robin swung round and looked at her. He didn't look very pleased either.

'A visitor?' he enquired sarcastically. 'I'd hardly put King down as being a visitor.'

'He's been very good to us, Robin,' Catherine said sharply. 'He was very nice to me when Gramps died and he's given both of us a week off. He didn't really need to do that at all, and you know it.'

'I'm sure he's got some ulterior motive,' Robin surmised churlishly. He was searching about frantically in the desk he had in his room, and Catherine eyed him crossly for a moment and then turned towards her own room.

'Anyway,' she said, 'Damon's coming back for me in two hours and I'll be off.'

'Damon?' Robin looked at her in surprise. 'Is that what you call him?'

'No.' She went quite pink. It had just slipped out because she thought of him like that now.

'He's dangerous,' Robin reminded her, suddenly serious and concerned. 'Don't forget that, Cath. It was you who said it first.'

But she had forgotten. She felt close to Damon, although it was all quite ridiculous. It was because she was staying with him, she told herself quickly. It was because of Ravenhall. When they were back in the offices in London this odd feeling of belonging would go.

When Damon came back for her in two hours exactly she had her cases packed, and this time she didn't much care whether she came back for the weekend or not. She and Robin had grown apart and Gramps had gone. What else was there? She might just as well get on with her career.

She glanced at Damon's face as he pulled away from the house, the car picking up speed as it sped along the street. Whatever career she had depended entirely upon Damon, and she knew for a fact that in spite of his kindness he suspected her as much as he had ever done.

He didn't speak very much, only when it was absolutely necessary, and the journey seemed to take longer than usual because she was so aware that he was sitting beside her and that his mind was working furiously over something that he would keep completely to himself. Once again he was dark and brooding, and she was surprised how lonely it made her feel.

Over the next couple of weeks when she was back at work she found to her dismay that his moods did not lift. He seemed to be watching her when she least expected it, coming suddenly into the room when she was working. It was as if the encounter with Robin had sharpened his antagonism again, and it made her very nervous. Her nervous ways seemed to make him even more suspicious. It was a circle of distrust that was never-ending.

When she had been back a few days he came into her office one afternoon with a cold glitter in his eyes.

'I'll be in for dinner tonight,' he informed her icily.

She didn't know why he was telling her that. He didn't have to inform her of his comings and goings; in fact he had not been in for dinner for several evenings.

'I thought I'd better tell you because we'll have a visitor,' he continued when she said nothing at all. 'Leonie is coming to dinner tonight, and in view of the rather strange happenings the last time she came I felt you ought to be warned.'

It brought it all back, and Catherine's face went pale. Yes, she had been phoning her grandfather then. She sprang up and went to stare out of the window, her shoulders tight.

'We're not going to have that problem now, though, are we?' she murmured unhappily. 'It was a once-only effort, because I won't be phoning Gramps again.'

There was a catch in her voice, and she heard him swear under his breath before he strode across to her, taking her slim shoulders in his hands and spinning her round to face him.

'You know I didn't mean that,' he said sharply. She just looked up at him, meeting his eyes, and his frown darkened. 'You probably thought I did after all,' he grated. 'Quite obviously you always think the worst of me.'

'Then that makes us equal,' Catherine pointed out miserably, 'because you always think the worst of me, don't you?'

Long, strong fingers tilted her chin, turning her face up.

'You have no idea what I think of you,' he assured her softly, and she found the amber eyes staring into hers again, hypnotising her. She shook herself free, turning away.

'It doesn't really matter. I just work for you.'

'You worked for me when you cried on my shoulder,' he reminded her, 'but it didn't seem to bother you then. You needed me.'

'I was upset,' Catherine said bitterly. 'Whoever had held me . . .'

'And now you're just upsetting yourself. You know I didn't think about your grandfather when I said that. It was just a thoughtless remark. I just wanted to warn you that we'd be having a guest for dinner.'

'There really is no need to include me,' Catherine advised him tightly. 'I'm quite happy to eat with Mrs Jarvis.'

He looked furious, and she was a bit anxious about the anger on his face.

'You'll do no such thing,' he snapped. 'You'll eat where I eat, and if you don't like Leonie you don't have to speak to her.'

'I don't care about her one way or the other,' Catherine said with equal sharpness. 'I hope you remember that. This is your house and she's your guest. I just happen to work here, and that's only because you *made* me come. I never wanted to come.'

She walked back to her desk, and after looking at her in irritation for a little while Damon walked out. Things actually seemed to be worse than they had ever been, and Catherine spent the rest of the day in deep gloom.

CHAPTER SIX

OVER the next few days Leonie became a frequent visitor. Never once did her attitude to Catherine soften, and Catherine didn't know whether Damon was inviting her deliberately or whether Leonie was inviting herself in order to keep her eye on Damon and Ravenhall Manor. It didn't seem to please him, though. He appeared to be growing more furious and darkly brooding as the days went by.

As it became warmer, Catherine began to enjoy the garden in her spare time. She would sometimes take a book out there to read, but more often than not she just could not help pottering about among the plants. She got to know the gardener, and the happy hours out there helped to fill in a lot of her spare time.

Damon's watchful mood had never relaxed, even though he left the house quite often. There were business meetings he had to attend, but the trip to Japan never materialised. Catherine suspected it was because he dared not leave her alone with the things in the office for that length of time, and, in spite of her determination to be uncaring, it hurt.

Walking under the trees one afternoon, she was shocked to realise that she now thought of Ravenhall Manor as home. It was impossible to imagine living anywhere else, and the recognition brought a burst of feeling that was almost fear. The awareness had grown in her over the time she had been here, but most of all it had grown since Damon had brought her back after her grandfather's death, and she realised that it was something to do with Damon himself.

However angry he was, however moody, she was used to seeing him. She was used to having breakfast at the same table, used to his unexpected arrival at any time and the swift glance of inspection he gave her whenever he came in.

Pretty soon it must dawn on him that she was not doing anything wrong at all, but, rather than making her feel any better, that thought made her more miserable. He would then quite likely get rid of her. She had never been in any doubt as to why she had got this job in the first place and why she was working at Ravenhall. When his suspicions were proved to be wrong, it would be the end.

Lost in the gloomy contemplation of this, she jumped nervously when Damon suddenly appeared in front of her. He had been out all morning and she had not expected him back until later. She knew he had several meetings in London, and she felt a new wave of anguish when she realised that he had probably come back early to catch her out. All he had caught her doing was wasting time in the garden.

'You look guilty,' he said wryly. 'Planning my early demise?'

'I never heard your car.' Catherine tried to pull herself together and meet his mocking eyes. She was breathlessly aware that he had lost some of the edge of hardness, and she was almost afraid to speak in case the golden eyes iced over again.

'I realised that. You were too deeply involved in your own thoughts.' He just stood looking at her, and she had to say something. As usual she spoke her thoughts out aloud.

'I was thinking you would probably want me to leave soon.'

'Were you?' He regarded her critically, his tawny eyes narrowed on her rather desperate face. 'Now that's a very strange conclusion. I don't recall ever saying anything to make you imagine that. In any case, I rather thought you wanted to stay. You seem settled in the house.'

'I assumed I was just here on some sort of trial,' Catherine said, hesitating to face him head-on when it came to it. She didn't feel like accusing him of suspecting her of espionage. 'And—and anyway, it would be stupid to become settled here, wouldn't it?'

'Why?' He looked at her seriously. 'You think *I'm* going to tell you to leave?'

'Sooner or later,' Catherine murmured. 'I—I don't feel too happy, and when you want me to leave...'

'I'm accustomed to reading expressions, and yours are usually transparent. You're looking particularly miserable just now, and that usually means you'd like to see me on Mars. I naturally took it that you were thinking about leaving, but don't put the blame on me. You'd better tell me right now if you're going, because I've got something for you.'

Catherine just stared up at him and he suddenly relaxed, taking her arm and helping her up on to the higher ground of the drive.

'I'll take it that your silence means you're undecided,' he said drily, 'so I'll press my advantage. I suppose it comes under the heading of bribery. You'll may fly into a rage, of course; one never knows.'

'I think I behave rather well,' Catherine muttered glumly, 'in the circumstances.'

'In the circumstances,' he agreed ironically. He turned her to face him and looked at her seriously. 'I don't want you to leave, Catherine, if that's what's worrying you. I need you here. I told you that right from the first.'

'It's *why* you need me here that's worrying.' She looked up at him anxiously, her face slightly flushed at his unexpectedly changed tone.

'For the same reason I brought you here in the first place.'

'But that was because...'

'Because what?' His hands moved to cup her face and his lips twisted wryly. 'I can guarantee you have no idea why I brought you here.' He looked into her eyes and then smiled. 'At any rate, you fit into the place. I'm sure if you go you'll haunt Ravenhall like a little dark-haired ghost; therefore I'm keeping you. As you're a real, live person I can order you about. As a ghost, you might ignore me.'

Catherine couldn't think of anything to say. She couldn't understand his tone, and for a few seconds she just stared back into those amber eyes. His hands slightly tightened, his gaze running slowly over her lips, and then he turned away almost abruptly.

'Let's get back to the present,' he murmured sardonically. 'You're trouble enough as a real person. As I told you, I've got something for you.'

'It's very kind, thank you,' Catherine said stiffly, and he shot her an amused glance.

'You've no idea what it is. It might be something terrible. You're certainly weird, Catherine Farrell.'

It wasn't that at all. She was still a little dazed, shaken by the way he had looked at her and even more shaken by her response to it, and she just kept quiet as he led her around the back of the house.

The old stable block had been turned into garages, and as they walked into the largest one Damon pointed to where a small car was parked neatly by the wall.

'That's what I brought you to see. I assume you can drive?'

'Of course!' Catherine just stood and looked at it. It was a Golf, a metallic silver, and even in the darkness of the garage she could see it was new.

'Who does it belong to?' she asked, confused as usual by Damon's way of going about things.

'It belongs to me. Sometimes I don't need to take the big car with me. When I don't, I take that. I find it quite exhilarating to drive after the comfort and smoothness of the Mercedes. While you're here, it's yours,' he finished quietly.

She spun round in astonishment.

'What do you mean?'

'I mean exactly what I said. It's yours while you're here. Since your grandfather died you've been trapped here. You never ask to go out anywhere. You're just quiet and subdued. There must be things you need, and there must be times when you want to go up to London or go back to your own house. That brother of yours seems extremely reluctant to fetch you. You now have a car. You don't need him.'

Yes, Robin was extremely reluctant to fetch her, and many a time she would have liked to go home unexpectedly to find out what he was up to. He phoned her from time to time and she phoned him, and she knew he had a lot on his mind, but she had no idea what it was.

She also felt guilty, as usual. Robin was alone. Robin had gone out as often as he could when Gramps was there, and she assumed he was doing the same thing now. All the same, she still had the feeling of responsibility.

'Do you really mean it?' Catherine looked up at Damon in the dim light, and he nodded.

'I rarely say things I don't mean. Whenever you want the car just take it. I told you, it's yours for as long as you want it.'

Catherine's face lit up with pleasure.

'You're very kind to me.' She smiled, and Damon was suddenly silent.

'In different circumstances I would probably be a lot kinder,' he told her softly, and she knew what he meant. He would be different if he didn't suspect her. But he did suspect her. She could see it on his face.

She turned away and walked over to the car.

'Sometimes I could go home in the evenings,' she said, anxious to get on to another subject.

'You can do whatever you like,' Damon assured her harshly. His voice had changed, and there was no longer any softness in him. He was thinking again about the reason for her being here. Considering the suspicions he had, he was more than kind. She looked across and smiled at him, and his expression softened a little.

'Come along,' he ordered. 'You look utterly entranced. Remind me to buy you a teddy bear.'

She didn't mind if he thought she was childish. He was trying to be nice, and she had to help him all she could.

As they were walking back towards the front of the house they both heard a car coming up the drive, and for one worrying moment Catherine thought it was Robin. The chances of him coming here were very slim, but she had this feeling that he was on the verge of trouble all the time, and she was expecting to hear about it almost daily.

It was not Robin's bright Ford that came into view, though; it was a dark green Jaguar, a car that she easily recognised because she had been in it herself. It belonged to Gordon Turner, and she assumed he had come to see Damon.

Damon obviously thought so too, but he didn't wait; he just went slowly up towards the house with Catherine, and as it happened they all arrived at the same time.

Damon and Catherine were at the steps just as the Jaguar stopped, and Gordon got out immediately.

To Catherine's surprise he didn't turn to Damon at all. He turned to her.

'So you still exist?' he asked with a smile. He ignored Damon, and Catherine felt nervous. He really was chancing his arm, coming into Damon's territory un-invited, unless it was important, but he had no briefcase in his hand and he seemed very reluctant to speak to Damon at all. When he did turn to Damon the smile was still on his face, but it was rather fixed.

'I came to see if Catherine was free this evening,' he announced, and she didn't have to turn round to know that Damon was immediately furious.

She assumed it was because an underling had tres-passed uninvited on to his territory. It was like storming the palace, and if Gordon had any sense he would have known it. She was astounded that he had the courage to come. He was showing a great deal of interest in her and, although it was rather flattering, at the moment it was also very worrying.

She could feel Damon seething, and she dared not look round. For a few moments in the garage he had been quite gentle. Now here was Gordon, and he was going to upset everything. Why on earth hadn't he phoned? It would have been so much more simple. He could have arranged to pick her up, but here he was, and there was nothing she could do about the trouble it would cause.

'Have you got anything for me?' Damon asked curtly, and Gordon shook his head.

'Not a thing.' He grinned very widely. 'I was hoping to take something away from you, actually.'

Damon just looked at him hard for a few seconds.

'Then I'll leave you to your social event,' he said acidly. He turned round and walked into the house, and the atmosphere trailing behind him was thunderous.

Catherine was annoyed. She didn't want to be at cross purposes with Damon, and although she liked Gordon she was not sufficiently interested to have her days here upset by his arrival. She turned on him straight away.

'Why on earth didn't you ring?' she asked. 'Why just come like this? You can tell he's not pleased.'

Gordon merely laughed.

'I bet he's not,' he surmised harshly. 'As a matter of fact I *have* rung, several times, but I've never been able to get you.'

'I didn't know.'

Catherine looked at him closely, not quite sure whether to believe him, but from the look on his face she knew it was true, and she was astounded when he said, 'Every time I rang Damon answered and told me that you were either not there or very busy.'

'Well, perhaps I wasn't there,' Catherine said very quickly. 'My grandfather died.'

'I know,' he said quietly. 'It must have been a terrible shock to you, Catherine. It wasn't then that I phoned, though. I knew what was happening, because everyone in the office knew. Your brother was away at the same time. We assumed that if Damon had given him a week off he would have done the same for you.'

'He did,' Catherine said. 'He was very kind to me.'

'Oh, he is kind,' Gordon said, looking at her out of the corner of his eyes, 'particularly to ladies.'

'There's nothing like that!' Catherine snapped. In other circumstances she would have been quite happy to see Gordon, but now she just wished he would go. 'Anyway, I expect you rang when I was having the week off. You must be mistaken.'

'I'm not. I rang after Robin returned to work and after I knew you were back here. It was always Damon who answered, and you were always unavailable. I asked if you could phone me back, but I notice you haven't.'

Catherine just stared at him. There was no doubt he was telling the truth, and he was looking at her in an odd sort of way that was embarrassing, as if something was going on here that she didn't want to tell him about.

'Well, I didn't know,' she confessed reluctantly. 'I'm sorry about that. I'll speak to Mr King about it and then maybe in future I'll get any messages.'

'Have you got the evening free?' Gordon persisted.

But Catherine didn't want to go anywhere. She was angry. For reasons best known to himself, Damon was quietly cutting her off. She could not understand why he had suddenly lent her a car if he wanted to isolate her, but no doubt it was part of this deep plan of his, and she could well do without his deep plans.

For a little while there he had lulled her into feeling that he cared sufficiently about her welfare to note that she had not been able to get out. What was he doing now—giving her enough rope to hang herself with?

'I'm not free this evening,' she said firmly, 'but I'll ring you.'

When Gordon had gone she marched straight in. She was going to tackle Damon now, and there was no use putting it off. For some reason or other he had not wanted her to go anywhere near Gordon, and she could only think that it was because he felt she might get information out of Gordon that she could use.

He was in his study, and she walked straight in with no hesitation. She was not going to stand for this. She was here at his instigation, but she was not a slave. She came in without knocking, and he looked up in surprise. This was not her usual way. Her cheeks were flushed, and he could see by the sparkle in her eyes that trouble was brewing.

He stood up slowly, watching her intently as he walked round the desk.

'How dare you cut me off from the outside world?' Catherine snapped. 'How dare you say that I'm either out or busy when I'm no such thing?' He didn't say a word, and she went on forcefully, 'I'm not a slave! It's because of you that I'm away from town, where I would have had my nights free and my weekends. I can go out wherever I wish and I can go when I wish, so long as it's not in working hours.'

Damon just went on looking at her. She could tell he was angry. His eyes had taken on that icy tawny look again, but she was too angry herself to care.

'I've just let you have a car for going where you wish,' he reminded her coldly. 'And let me point out to you that I pay you more for being here in the lap of luxury.'

'I'd rather earn less and be free,' she seethed. 'Gordon thinks you're hiding me. I felt an utter fool just now. It's as if you're pretending that I'm not here at all. It's no use pretending, because everyone knows where I am.'

'Oh, so do I,' Damon rasped. He marched forward and towered over her, glaring down at her. 'I know you're here every minute.'

'Yes, and I know *why* I'm here,' Catherine raged. She was not about to be intimidated. She tilted her chin and stared at him very angrily. 'You think I'm up to something. You think I'm going to do something nasty and surreptitious behind your back, and you're making quite sure that you don't turn your back on me at all. That's why you haven't been away to Japan, isn't it?'

Damon grabbed her. Before she knew what was happening he had her shoulders in a very tight grip, and he was furious. She could see rage on his face, but Catherine was in a rage herself. He had never resorted to physically restraining her before, and she completely forgot who he was and how dangerous he was.

'Let go of me!' She lashed out at him as hard as she could, and he moved his head, avoiding her blows easily, but she was too angry to stop, too angry to see the danger on his face. She still lashed out at him, and he subdued her easily. His arm went tightly around her waist, his other hand fastening harshly in the long black hair, tightening, and jerking her head up. There was a white line of fury along his lips, and for a moment he held her and said nothing, jerking her head painfully when she refused to stop.

It did not bring her to her senses. She was hurt, angry, and she still struggled, rejecting the cold fury that she saw on his face. He tightened his hold in her hair, forcing her face up until it was very close to his.

'Stop this!' he ordered, every muscle in him tense with anger, but she struggled furiously, ignoring his growl of rage, and his control of his temper snapped.

She knew what was coming even before it had happened. His mouth fastened on hers, tight and hard. Even so, the main cause of her sudden fear was the response he evoked in her, something she had never felt before.

A breathless melting sensation seemed to spread all the way through her, although he was doing nothing but threaten. When he let her go she was trembling all over, and she stared at him with wide grey eyes, terrified of how she was feeling.

'Damn you, Catherine!' He glared down at her, and she just looked back at him, her face completely white.

'I want to leave,' she said in a trembling voice. 'I want to leave now. There's no need for me to stay here as a hostage for Robin. I don't have to worry about my grandfather now. I don't have to take care of him. I've got no obligations any more.'

She remembered then, and all the misery came back in one great sweeping wave. Damon had hurt her, not physically, but by his attitude. Gradually she had found herself being drawn closer to him, and now he had treated her like this. That, added to the feelings that she had when she remembered her grandfather and remembered that there was absolutely no purpose in struggling with this job any longer, forced all the misery back with a big burning rush.

She burst into tears, unable to stop, shakily covering her face with her hands, but Damon pulled them away and reached out for her.

'Let me go!' she sobbed, but he pulled her towards him relentlessly.

'Don't, Catherine. Don't cry.' This time there was no violence in him, and once again she was back in his arms, but it was very different. 'Oh, Catherine,' he murmured. 'You really bring out the worst in me. Why the hell did you fly at me like that? You know what I'm like.'

'I don't care,' she sobbed. 'And I'm only crying because I'm angry. I wouldn't give you the satisfaction of seeing me really cry.'

Damon's hand slid round the back of her neck, his thumb tilting her face. 'It wouldn't give me any satisfaction at all,' he said almost bitterly. 'It just drives me to comforting you, and that's something I can very well do without.'

'I don't want comfort!' She looked up desperately, and his face was very close, his eyes on her trembling mouth, and this time there was no fear when the hard lips closed over her own. This time it was the most mind-stopping thing that had ever happened to her. It was an excitement and wonder beyond compare. She seemed to be swept up into the clouds, weightless and drifting, as Damon's lips probed her own, and any desire to fight him left her completely.

For timeless seconds she hung there, dreamily submissive, feather-light in his arms, and then a great joy came sweeping through her, surging like a fire out of control. It was a joy she had never felt before, and her hands touched his face, searching the silken rasp of his skin, as her arms wound around his neck in glorious acceptance of the conquest. Damon eased away impatiently, but her arms tightened, her face tilted up to his.

'Oh...' She breathed her wonder and delight into his mouth, and the response it brought was swift and powerful. His mouth crushed hers again, forcing her lips apart, as his arms gathered her up to hold her against the hard force of his chest. It was ruthless, taking her over completely, but Catherine simply sank into it, languid and trembling, eagerly accepting the dominance. She was still totally lost when he drew back and looked down into her enchanted eyes. Her face was radiant and she stared bewitched into eyes that watched her steadily.

'More, Catherine?' he enquired, and she knew he was mocking her, contemptuous, taunting, the Damon that she had grown to know.

She had simply let him kiss her in any way he liked, and even now she could not move to wrench herself free. It was Damon who let her go; his hands fell away from her and he stepped back.

'I'm sorry,' he muttered. 'I suppose you needed kissing, though perhaps not like that. Next time you're in need of comfort we'll give Gordon a call, shall we?'

Catherine couldn't answer. She was still standing there when the telephone rang, and he turned round immediately to pick it up as if nothing had happened between them. She knew straight away who it was, even before Damon said the name. It was Leonie, and Catherine ran out of the room in distress. She made her way to her own bedroom and shut the door. She was still trembling and there was this strange burning feeling inside her, a melting in the pit of her stomach.

She told herself that she was a complete fool. She knew that Damon was playing some deep game of his own. She knew he was trying to trap her. She could not understand why he had kissed her that second time, but she knew why he had kissed her the first time—sheer rage. She felt she had to get away right now, this minute. It was dangerous for her here, and she would never be able to face him again.

She didn't have a lot of choice. A few seconds later Damon knocked on her door, and when she refused to answer he opened it and came to stand inside. He looked as if nothing had happened between them. He was back to simply being her boss, cool and efficient.

'I'm afraid you'll have to work late tonight,' he informed her briskly. 'Something's come up. If you'll come down to your office we'll get started.'

He turned round and walked out, behaving as if nothing had happened at all, and she could tell from the look on his face that that was how he intended to behave in the future. The fact that it had shaken her so deeply did not matter to Damon. He didn't care about anyone, and he certainly didn't care about her.

Catherine went down to her office, and Damon was already there, searching through the letters that had suddenly come in on the fax. She could see that he was going to ignore the whole episode between them, and she decided that if he could then she could too.

'There's been a lot of movement in the financial markets over this past week,' he said crisply. 'It's suddenly come to a head. We've got to act fast on this particular one.' He put some papers on to her desk. 'Sort these out and we'll take it from there.'

That was all he was going to say. He turned towards the door to go back to his own study, and Catherine glanced down at the papers.

'Foster and Brown?' The sound of her voice stopped him, and he turned back to look at her. 'But I thought you said they weren't worth your while.'

He stared at her for a few minutes, his eyes narrowed.

'You've got a very good memory,' he said softly. There was that menacing attitude about him again, almost sinister.

'It's not a day I'm likely to forget,' Catherine pointed out sharply. 'That was the day when you almost savaged me when I came for the interview.' He had almost savaged her earlier, and when she said that she was very pleased to see a streak of colour come across his face. So he had not taken it as lightly as she had imagined ... But she could see suspicion back immediately.

'I heard you mention the name then and I haven't forgotten it,' she continued. 'I just thought you weren't interested, that's all. Sorry I spoke.' He went on looking at her and then shrugged. Evidently he had not seen on her face what he had expected to see, and Catherine knew what that was—guilt.

'Things change fast in the money world,' he muttered. 'Sort those out and I'll get on the phone. Bring them through as soon as they're ready.'

They were working for the rest of the day, and Catherine was amused to find that when Leonie rang Damon was quite short with her. He was doing what he liked to do, stalking some firm, and at this moment he had no time for Leonie at all.

It was quite late before they finished. Mrs Jarvis came in several times to ask about their dinner, but she hardly got an answer, and finally Damon told her to bring a tray for both of them, and they ate in his study. The phone was constantly ringing, and it was about nine o'clock at night before they finished. Throughout the time, Damon had never shown any sign that he even remembered the kisses of earlier, and Catherine began to think she had dreamed it all.

She collected the trays and took them to the kitchen and then came back to stand in the doorway of his study.

'Have we finished now?'

Damon looked up as she spoke, putting the phone down and gazing at her steadily. 'Yes, thank you. You look tired. Better get off to bed.'

She nodded, turning to leave, but he called to her and she stopped, not looking round.

'Catherine, I'm sorry I savaged you—again.' An apology from Damon was utterly unexpected, and she half turned, expecting to see some derision on his face. He was serious, though, and of course she didn't know what to say then. 'I'm not really used to someone like you,' he went on quietly. 'You're quite outside the world I know.'

'Well, I have humble beginnings,' Catherine reminded him wryly, suddenly amused by his rather troubled expression.

'I didn't mean that!' He looked cross, and then his eyes narrowed at her wry looks. 'You damned well know it too, you little cat.' He leaned back in his chair and stretched wearily. 'I live in a hard world, Catherine; I even built it myself. Having you here is—strange.'

'Then let me go,' Catherine said brightly. She suddenly had the feeling of having the upper hand, a most unusual feeling with Damon. 'If I make you uneasy in your hard world, then just tip me out of it.'

'I said that having you here was strange,' he growled. 'I never confessed to being stupid. Go to bed before we have another fight.'

She went to bed with very mixed feelings. Damon was unreachable; she had known that for a long time. She also knew now that she wanted to reach him, and it was utter folly, something she had better put completely out of her mind.

She hadn't really understood everything that had gone on this evening, but she knew enough about the King Group now to know that Damon was acting differently over this particular take-over. It was nothing to do with her, but it worried her almost instinctively.

He was spinning some sort of a web, and she dreaded to think who would be caught in it. For the first time ever he had given her a lot of information, and she wondered if it had been part of his dreaded plan. She felt like locking herself in her room and sealing the door so that she could not in any way be a suspect.

CHAPTER SEVEN

IT WAS two or three days later that Robin decided to take his wild chance. The information came his way by accident, he snapped it up, and of course he was caught. Catherine knew nothing about it until Damon came back from London one day and came straight into her office.

'I think you'd better come with me,' he said, looking at her seriously. 'That brother of yours is in deep trouble.'

She sprang to her feet, her face white straight away. She didn't know what it was, but she knew that Robin had been up to something for some time, and she had been dreading hearing about it.

'What sort of trouble?' she asked anxiously, and Damon told her.

'Selling information. God knows how it fell into his hands, but it did, and he wasn't slow to do something with it.'

'He wouldn't!' she gasped, but Damon shook his head.

'He's already confessed. He's also told me that you had nothing to do with it.'

Catherine just looked at him bleakly. Yes, she had been right all the way along the line. That was why she was here. She turned away miserably.

'I'll get my bag.'

'Catherine!' Damon tried to speak to her, but she didn't want to listen. She was far too hurt for any words, and she was worried about Robin. She had no idea what Damon would do. She had no idea how much against the law this sort of thing was. She felt like a babe at the side of all these people who passed millions between

115

them, and she realised that she did not fit in any way into Damon's life. Having her here must certainly be strange, as he had said.

'It's all right,' she said quietly. 'Whatever it is, I'm sure Robin and I will be able to deal with it.'

Damon didn't take her up to the big offices in London. He took her back home, and that was even more worrying.

'Why are we here?' Catherine looked at him anxiously as he pulled up outside her house.

'We're here because your brother is here,' Damon told her grimly. 'I don't want any trouble in the office, and very few people know about this. I know, you know, and Turner knows.'

'Gordon knows?'

Damon's face darkened with anger at the sound of the name.

'Yes! He told me immediately. That's part of his job. You're lucky he's the boyfriend or it might have spread further.'

Catherine opened her mouth to protest that Gordon certainly was not her boyfriend, but she thought better of it. Damon looked very angry again, and there was still the matter of Robin to be faced. She always came off badly in any argument with Damon in any case.

Robin was in the sitting-room, looking very pale. He had obviously been told to go there and wait, and that was exactly what he was doing.

'You damn fool,' Damon growled as soon as they saw him. 'What made you even imagine for one minute that you would get away with it? There are no short cuts to making money. Even if you had succeeded, what did you expect to do with such a paltry sum—live wildly for a couple of months?'

Robin said nothing. He was obviously in a state of trauma, too shocked to answer, but Catherine answered for him.

'He intended to launch out into his dream,' she said quietly. 'Isn't that what it was, Rob?'

Robin nodded, and Damon spun round and looked at her.

'Dream? What are you talking about?'

Catherine almost collapsed on to the settee. She folded her hands in her lap and looked up at Damon. There was no way of getting Robin out of this, so Damon might as well know the whole truth.

'Robin is a very good musician,' she told him calmly. 'When he went to college he wanted to be an accountant, but he joined a group there. He's been playing ever since, at nights in clubs, going out further over the weekends. It's the big interest of his life, the only interest.'

She glanced across at Robin and shook her head sadly. How foolish people were sometimes, and that included herself with the way she felt about Damon.

'Robin wants to be a pop star,' she continued softly. 'That's the only reason he joined your firm, because of Crown Records.'

She could see that Damon was stunned.

'A *pop* star?' Considering it was Damon's hobby to deal with Crown Records, he sounded utterly astounded that someone should want to perform. He turned to Robin angrily. 'Why, you damn young fool, don't you know we've had our eye on you for some time? You're bright! We're always looking for people like that. You would have gone a long with the firm.' He put his hands in his pockets and paced about. 'What the hell am I going to do with you now?' he rasped.

'Whatever you think,' Robin said quietly. 'It's not the sort of thing I'm likely to do again. Anyway, obviously I'm no good at it.'

'That's not a very reassuring attitude.' Damon spun round and frowned at him.

'You know what I mean.'

'How the hell do I know what you mean!' Damon snapped. 'I can't reckon you up at all.' If Catherine hadn't been so anxious she would have smiled. It seemed that anyone who didn't come from Damon's hard world was strange. Now Robin was included.

'Cath's been warning me all the way along the line,' Robin muttered.

'Has she?' Damon queried darkly, and Robin's head shot up at the sinister tone.

'Cath didn't know what I was planning. She would have gone mad. What I mean is, she's been trying to get me just to carry on with my normal career. I should have listened to her.'

'Yes, you should,' Damon said acidly, 'but that's beside the point. What do we do with you now?'

'I don't know.' Robin shook his head, looking down at the floor, and Damon paced around for a few minutes more. He glanced at Catherine, but she looked away. She didn't want to look at him. Once again he had shown how much he distrusted her, and, even though she had always known it, it hurt more now.

Damon stopped pacing as he made his mind up.

'You're suspended for a week,' he told Robin coldly. 'I've got to think this one out.'

Robin looked up, even more shocked than Catherine felt. He had expected no mercy, and he wasn't sure what this was.

'Whatever you decide to do, Cath had nothing to do with this,' he insisted urgently.

'I know that,' Damon assured him icily. 'Even if you hadn't been telling me over and over since this happened, I would have known. There's no way she could have got hold of that information. You did it all by yourself.'

'Cath's never had anything to do with anything,' Robin insisted. 'Her only concern has been about Gramps and me. It's too late about Gramps now, and obviously I'm a rotter.'

'Stop feeling sorry for yourself!' Damon snarled. 'Maybe that's what's wrong with you.' He looked steadily at Robin for a moment. 'Maybe you should dabble your toe in a bit of hot water after all,' he mused. 'It might just do you some good. Let me think about it. Meanwhile, keep your nose out of trouble and out of the office.'

'What will they think?' Robin asked.

'They'll think what I damn well tell them to think, and if they don't then they'll have enough sense to keep quiet about it!' Damon grated. 'All you have to do is worry about me!'

'I—I'll make you some tea, Rob,' Catherine said, but Damon grasped her wrist and jerked her to her feet.

'Oh, no, you won't,' he announced. 'He takes care of himself. Mothering has obviously done him no good at all. He's got a week in which to grow up, and he can start now. What I decide to do with him depends entirely on how far *up* he grows.'

Catherine had no alternative. She looked back at Robin, and he shrugged his shoulders. He didn't look as miserable as when they came in, but he was looking extremely puzzled, and who would not be? She had no idea what Damon was going to do or what hot water he was going to allow Robin to dabble in. She never got the chance to talk to Robin at all, though. Damon just moved her to the door and out to his car.

'I should stay. . .' she began, but Damon didn't even bother to answer. She was in the passenger seat before she knew it, and he took off speedily.

'You should leave him on his own to think things out. If he hasn't had the opportunity to think things out before he's got a whole week to do it now. We'll see what happens.'

Catherine didn't know whether it was a good idea or a bad one. She did know that it was totally unexpected. They drove along in silence, and Damon suddenly grunted, 'Damn! It wasn't what I expected.'

'No,' Catherine agreed bitterly. 'You expected me to do it. You thought I wanted to join the firm so that I could pass information on to Robin. You were even stunned that I wasn't in on this. Anyway, you can see he's not very good at stealing. It was just a wild idea that he carried through very badly.'

'I know,' Damon agreed, 'and for your information. . .'

He stopped there, saying nothing else, and when Catherine looked at him his face was quite closed. She knew she was not going to get another thing out of him, but, mulling it over, she decided that Robin had been very lucky to make a mess of things.

If he had done things more slickly and got away with it he would probably have gone on to greater things, and sooner or later Damon would have caught him. There was no doubt in her mind whatsoever about that. Where this left her, she didn't know.

For the next few days she was completely on edge, waiting for Damon to announce his decision, but when it came it was something completely unexpected. He walked into her office and looked at her for a moment before saying,

'Get your brother on the phone. Tell him to come over here now.'

'Over here?' Catherine felt this was even worse. Damon was summoning Robin to Ravenhall, and that must be very bad.

'Yes, over here!' Damon snapped. 'This is where we are, Miss Farrell. That young fool has had enough people running around after him. This time he can come to us!'

He walked out, and Catherine sat down to recover from her surprise. It was unusual for Damon to speak like that—'we' and 'us'. Apparently she was to be included in anything he had to say. It didn't make her feel any less anxious, and she phoned Robin right away, praying he had not had an attack of defiance and gone out. He hadn't, and from the tone of his voice he felt as nervous as she did at this order to appear at Ravenhall.

She couldn't do a thing after that. Damon stayed in his own study and Catherine spent most of the time looking out of the window, watching anxiously for Robin. It seemed like ages before she saw his car come up the drive, and this time he was in no hurry. There was no tearing up to the door, and she knew exactly how he felt. If it hadn't been so serious it would have been laughable. He had spent months wanting Damon to notice him, and now he would have given anything to be invisible.

She met him at the door, ready to take him to Damon's study, but they never got there. Damon came out and signalled them both to the drawing-room.

'Sit down,' he ordered as they both hovered together nervously like conspirators, and Robin sat in a chair, perched on the very edge, waiting for fate to overtake him. 'You too,' Damon growled as Catherine still stood there nervously. When she didn't move, he made an impatient noise and grasped her wrist, pulling her down to the settee with him. 'Will you both stop behaving as if you've been invited to your own execution?' he rasped. 'I haven't actually planned to kill either of you!'

To Catherine though it sounded as if he might have the idea lurking at the back of his mind, and she hardly dared to breathe. She was sitting close to Damon too, and that was quite devastating, apart from the fact that it must appear to Robin that he was in front of some sort of private court. She had to admit that he looked terrified.

'You can have your chance,' Damon told Robin, after staring at him disconcertingly for a while. 'I think you're probably mad, but if you want a go at the world of entertainment, I'll launch you.'

Robin just sat and stared, quite clearly stunned, and Catherine couldn't believe what she had just heard.

'Do you mean——?' Robin began, and Damon interrupted ruthlessly.

'I mean exactly what I say. You can have an audition, and if you're any good I'll launch you into the world you're so crazy about, although it seems to me that you're simply crazy. For a person with nothing on their mind but performing, you've done remarkably well at your real job. It makes me wonder just how good you would have been if you'd put your whole mind to it.'

'Suppose I fail the audition?' Robin asked with a diffidence that quite shook Catherine.

'Then it's back to work with no further nonsense,' Damon informed him grimly.

'You mean I could come back into the firm?' Robin sounded astonished, and Catherine felt much the same. She had never expected Damon to show any kind of mercy with anyone, especially with someone who had planned to steal from him.

'I do. And I would prefer it if you said the King Group. I don't particularly like to feel that I head a criminal organisation,' Damon pointed out drily. 'I can fix the audition up for this week,' he added.

'If it's all the same to you, I'd rather not,' Robin said hesitantly. 'I've been having a good think, and I'd rather stay at my job. If I've got a future, I should stick with it. So far performing has been fun. I'm not so sure it would be fun if it was all I ever did. It would probably be a bind.'

Catherine could hardly believe her ears, but Damon sat back and smiled with ironic satisfaction.

'So you *did* use the time to sort yourself out?' he queried wryly. 'I hoped you would, but I must confess I didn't exactly bank on it. You're twenty-five,' he pointed out more seriously, leaning forward and fixing Robin with those amber eyes. 'You've got a career and you're damned good at it. Stick with it and make something of yourself. Make music for fun, because believe me, it's hard out there.'

'So what do I do now?' Robin asked. Catherine had the funny feeling that she had missed a bit of this. She had just heard Robin give up the chance he had been dreaming of, and there was no mistaking Damon's satisfaction.

'You get back to the office,' Damon ordered briskly. 'It seems to me that what with one thing and another you've had enough time off to last for a while. Don't expect a further bunch of favours.'

Robin went red and looked very uncomfortable.

'I expect they know...?'

'They don't,' Damon assured him. 'I stamped on speculation instantly. You can say you've been doing something private for me. Tell them you had dinner at Ravenhall; that should convince them.' He looked extremely pleased with himself, quite amused, and when Mrs Jarvis walked past the door he called out that there would be one more for dinner.

'I take it that you won't object to our guest this time?' he asked, slanting a golden glance at Catherine. 'With a bit of luck, you might even manage to talk.'

Catherine blushed, and Robin looked from one to the other in surprise. Now that he had recovered from fright and shock, he was obviously sensing an atmosphere. He was also noticing that Catherine was sitting very close to Damon. He mentioned it as he was going home.

'Is something going on between you, Cath?' he asked as she went to the car with him.

'Only constant arguments,' she said quickly. 'Damon is the sort of person you can't fathom out.' He didn't look too sure, and Catherine was glad to wave him off. It was a worry out of her mind, at any rate. She was still a little stunned by the outcome, but she was quite sure that things would work out well. Damon seemed to have gathered Robin into the fold, and she had the feeling that he did that very rarely. If anyone could be said to be a loner, it was Damon, in spite of Leonie Saddler.

When she went back inside, Damon was still sitting there with a glass of brandy in his hand, and she knew she couldn't just go off to bed without thanking him. She had no idea how he would take thanks, though, and she hesitated at the door of the drawing-room.

'"Come into my parlour",' he murmured derisively. 'I'm not in the mood to eat you, so you're quite safe.'

'I just wanted to thank you,' Catherine managed, hovering by the door. 'I never expected you to be so kind to Robin. He doesn't exactly deserve it.'

'Probably not,' he murmured, looking across at her with an unreadable expression on his face. 'I doubt if he'll stray again, though, so ultimately I win. He'll be loyal, and he certainly is good. Of course, he did have an advantage from the first. He's your brother.'

'I would have thought that was a disadvantage,' Catherine muttered, looking away. 'I'm not high-powered enough to be your PA and I'm well aware of it. Here, at Ravenhall, I can cope well enough, but if we were back in London...'

'But we're not back in London,' he reminded her, standing and putting his glass down. 'In any case, I wouldn't think of taking you back there. I never intended to.' He gave her a crooked smile. 'Your post is filled, actually, Miss Farrell.'

'What do you mean?' Catherine looked at him tragically. Was this where he told her she could just go?

'I mean that a very efficient lady now occupies your former desk. I had her picked out long before Judith left.'

'Then why...?'

'I had other plans for you,' he reminded her. 'You were always going to be here. As it happens, you fit in well. I like the arrangement.'

'You—you still want me here?' she asked in a puzzled voice, and he looked at her with suddenly serious eyes.

'I still want you here,' he said quietly. 'In fact, if you wanted to go, I really think you would have to fight your way out.'

'But what am I?' Catherine wanted to know, and he walked across and smiled ironically into her worried eyes.

'You're a very *personal* assistant. It's a luxury I've never had before.' She knew he was laughing at her, and she knew that nothing with Damon was ever straightforward. She turned away fretfully, wishing she had gone. off to bed and never started this; now she wouldn't be able to sleep for puzzling it over.

'I don't understand you,' she complained quietly, and he caught her shoulder, turning her back and looking down at her with the derision still in his eyes.

'Of course you do,' he insisted. 'I'm rotten all the way through. I hunt people, ruin firms, destroy things. You've always thought that, haven't you?'

'I don't now,' Catherine assured him, almost whispering. 'I'm beginning to understand how things work.'

'Don't try to understand too much,' he warned. 'Any day now I might change my mind about you.'

Next day the news broke that the King Group were planning a take-over of Foster and Brown, and Catherine came down to breakfast to find Damon reading the business news. He tossed the paper across to her, folded back at the place, but he said nothing. She remembered that normally nobody knew what was happening until Damon had things sewn up, and this was not sewn up yet by any means. The news had been leaked, and it certainly was not Robin this time.

'So now we know,' Damon said softly, watching her. She thought immediately that he meant her, but she was too upset to defend herself. 'Somebody in the office is wheeling and dealing,' he went on quietly, and Catherine was astonished to see a smile on his face. She would have thought he would be furious.

'But I don't think it's funny,' she protested, and he looked at her levelly.

'Neither do I.'

'You still think it's me?'

'The hell I do. I *know* it's not you, Catherine; I've always known.'

She stared at him wide-eyed, too surprised to be relieved.

'But I thought you brought me here to... You said you had plans.'

'So I do,' he said. 'But not plans to put you in gaol. Poor little Catherine, did you think I was hunting you all this time?'

Catherine didn't know what to say. He was taunting again, looking at her with mocking amber eyes.

'I've had my suspicions for a long time,' he went on. 'Your brother's activities rather stunned me, but there's no way he can have access to high information, and I doubt if he'd know what to do with it if he got it. There are always people hanging around trying to find things out, and I suppose one of them tackled Robin, but he's not very good at it, is he?'

To her astonishment Damon was grinning, and she shook her head. She could hardly say that Robin was good at it.

'I think we've caught the big fish this time, though,' Damon continued. 'All I have to do now is backtrack and find out where the information landed.' He suddenly stood up to go. 'I really *am* hunting this morning. I'll see you later. Hold the fort.'

She just went on staring at him and then jumped up to follow him to the door.

'If we get any calls about this——' she began, and he spun round fast, frowning at her.

'You know nothing whatever!' he snapped, and she glared up at him, irritated by his sudden change of mood.

'I wasn't asking if it would be all right to issue a statement,' she snapped back. 'I just wondered what story you're putting out. Do you want "No comment" or "Mind your own business"?'

He grinned again and stepped back towards her.

'How about, "Mr King is not available at the moment"? You can say it in a terrified little voice.'

'I'll go and practise!' Catherine turned away impatiently, but he took hold of her arm and spun her back towards him, catching her in his arms as she turned.

'You do that, Miss Farrell,' he advised, laughing down at her, and to her great surprise he dropped a kiss on her parted lips. It was quick, warm and lingered just for a second, as if he was tasting her. When he lifted his head Catherine felt nothing but cross. Once again, he was playing with her feelings. He probably knew exactly how she felt about him and as usual he was laughing at her.

'Do you always kiss the hired help goodbye?' she asked angrily as he let her go.

'Of course not!' He walked to the door and looked back at her tauntingly. 'Mrs Jarvis is a respectable widow, and the cleaner is at least eighty. That just leaves you, and as I'm in an exuberant mood you just chased after me at the right time.'

'I did not chase after you!' Catherine stormed, but all she got was a mocking grin.

'Then work it into your schedule,' he advised. To her amazement he winked at her and walked out. For somebody whose plans had been thwarted, he was certainly light-hearted. Catherine just stood there staring after him, never moving, even when the Mercedes pulled away from the door.

He was hunting somebody and enjoying doing it. Whoever it was, he was going to enjoy catching them too. There was no doubt in her mind about that. It almost seemed personal to him. She gave a little shiver. She was glad it wasn't Robin and absolutely delighted that it was not her, because she knew that when Damon found out that someone he trusted had betrayed him and betrayed the firm he would be utterly ruthless.

Of course, the light-hearted kiss had meant nothing, but all the same she was singing under her breath as she finished breakfast and went into her office. When the expected enquiries came she almost laughed into the phone.

'Mr King is not available at the moment,' she managed solemnly. Not for the life of her could she summon up any terror. She was just too happy. When Robin phoned from work at lunchtime she was so bright and breezy that he commented on it.

'Of course I'm happy,' she lied cheerfully. 'You've got your job back, and Damon thinks you're good at it.'

'I've just seen him,' Robin told her enthusiastically. 'He actually came across to find me. It made a sensation. He shook my hand as he left and he did it deliberately, to make sure that nobody knew about my problem. He was in a very funny mood, though, but I don't think anybody knew it but me. They were all too busy trying to hear what he was saying, and they didn't manage it.'

'What did he actually say?' Catherine wanted to know, and Robin started to laugh.

'He said, "Watch your step!" in a very low, threatening voice.'

Catherine smiled to herself as Robin ended the call. Yes, she could believe it. That sounded just like Damon, but she was grateful to him. His presence at the office, speaking to Robin, would have cleared away any doubts that people had. He was keeping his word even in the midst of his hunting trip. She wondered if he would tell her who he suspected. Probably not. He kept most things to himself.

When he came back the buoyant mood seemed to have gone to some extent, and Catherine knew he was not about to confide in her at all. It was disappointing, but only what she had expected.

She did not expect the words he said later, though. She was just coming out of her room, and Damon met her in the passage.

'I've given Mrs Jarvis the evening off,' he told her abruptly. 'Get changed and we'll go out.'

'Out?' She turned to look at him, her grey eyes enormous. It was the last thing she had expected to hear.

'Out,' he murmured, his gaze skimming her face. 'The opposite of in. I can explain more fully if you're having trouble with the word.'

'It—it's just that I never expected...' Her words were said in a breathless manner that brought a quirky smile to his lips.

'Perhaps it's time you had higher expectations for yourself. It seems to me that you've spent the better part of your twenty-four years worrying about your brother. He's back in harness, and he's definitely not invited. I know you want to go. Therefore, get changed. I'll wait in the drawing-room.'

He walked off, and she was left torn between two warring emotions—the joy of going out with Damon, and the irritation of his supreme self-assurance. He thought he could twist her round his little finger. Well, he could, but there was no need for him to make it obvious that he knew.

He didn't choose the sort of place she expected at all. After a silent drive to London he seemed to be weaving in and out of streets for a long time, and when they arrived the place looked very quiet and dark to Catherine. His silence as they drove had quite unnerved her, and she had been dreading some brilliant place where people who knew Damon would look askance at her.

Once inside, though, she found the restaurant very upmarket but very old-fashioned.

'I'm told they used to have tea-dances here not too long ago,' Damon remarked, seeing her intrigued expression. 'Of course, they may do still, but I never get the chance to find out. It's drawing the more world-weary at the moment—no disco, no strobe lights, just a meal and a glide round the floor.'

'That suits me,' Catherine assured him cheerfully, 'although I didn't realise I was world-weary.'

'It creeps up on you.' She found him actually smiling down at her, and as he escorted her to their table, his hand warm against her back, a delicious feeling swept over her. She felt safe, comfortable and, for the moment, very happy.

Halfway through the meal Damon suddenly looked across at her and leaned back in his chair.

'Heard from your brother?' he asked quietly, and she had a moment of anxiety. Would he start suspecting Robin again now that he was back at work? Had he really meant it when he said he had never suspected her?

'Take your time,' Damon added drily. 'I know it was a difficult question.'

'He rang me this afternoon.' She blushed furiously, and he looked at her intently, as he often did. 'He was grateful to you for making the effort to see him,' she continued hurriedly.

'Not too grateful, I hope. I had several reasons for going in there.'

He was looking sardonic again, and Catherine's feeling of ease began to melt away. There was a slight menace in the atmosphere again, a menace that had drained away over the past few days. Once again she was on edge, and it came to her mind that he had told her quite specifically that he had another personal assistant. She was still only part of some obscure plan.

She looked down into her wine, avoiding his eyes.

'Anyway, it made him feel less vulnerable,' she murmured.

'Now perhaps you can get on with your own life,' he pointed out quietly. 'I told you he was OK, and I meant it. Think about yourself.'

'I don't know why you imagine I don't,' Catherine said crisply. 'I have plenty of time to think about myself, in any case. I'm not exactly ancient.'

'No.' He stood almost abruptly, his expression closing. 'Let's dance.'

She knew she had annoyed him. She was always doing that, with no idea how it happened. The wonderful peace had gone because Damon had taken it away, and out on the floor they mingled with everyone else, but now she felt alone, tight inside and fairly hopeless.

It was easy dancing with Damon. He danced well, and Catherine found it no strain at all. She was light as a feather, matching her steps to his, and after a few minutes Damon gave a low laugh.

'I have an urge to lift you and swirl you around,' he said softly, amusement in his voice. 'You'd probably just float off.'

'I wouldn't. I'd hang on tightly.' She smiled up at him, her eyes long and shimmering, clear and grey. She was glad to have him back to smiling, and for a second he looked back at her, his gaze moving over her smiling mouth, before he stared out rather grimly over her head.

'Why do I constantly irritate you?' she asked quietly.

'Probably because you're the exact opposite of me,' he grated. 'Or maybe it's because you frequently remind me of how young you are.'

'There's not a lot I can do about that.' She gave a rather tragic sigh. 'You've got a real PA now. You could send me back to my own house.'

'Forget it!' he snapped, instantly angered. 'I need you.'

'I can't think what for. I irritate you, and as I'm no longer under suspicion there's really no need to inflict that sort of punishment on yourself,' Catherine said frustratedly. All it gained for her was a grunt of annoyance, and she found herself pulled closer as his hands tightened painfully on her waist.

'Be quiet. You're ruining my evening.'

She opened her mouth to tell him that it had been his idea in the first place and that he could take her back, but something about him advised her to say nothing. He was dark and brooding and he didn't look as if he would take kindly to any argument.

He kept her out on the floor, and after a while she relaxed again. She liked dancing, and with Damon it was wonderful. His hand was warm against her back, the warmth finding its way to her skin through the thin silk of her dress, and shivers began to run down her spine. She wanted to be even closer, and her cheeks flushed at the thought.

'I'd like to take the car and do some shopping this week,' she said in a breathless rush, trying to take her mind off Damon and his nearness.

'Whenever you want. You don't have to ask me, although I'll take you shopping if you want to go into London. Don't expect any help if you're buying clothes, though. I'm not much good at choosing clothes for the female of the species.'

'Don't you buy clothes for Miss Saddler?' The words were out before she could stop them, and she knew it was a mistake of major proportions as she felt him stiffen with anger. He didn't even bother to answer, and Catherine kept her face well hidden as she bit into her lip, berating herself for her inability to hold her tongue.

She had always been diplomatic; it was just that she seemed to see him with Leonie Saddler every time she let herself be off guard. Now he would take her back to her seat and take her home as soon as possible, and it was her own fault.

'Oh, Catherine!' After a second he gave another of those dark, low laughs, and she realised that he was holding her more gently, his hand moving over her back, arching her closer. 'You blurt out every thought that comes into your head, don't you? I'm not sure what to do with you.'

'Perhaps you'd better take me home,' Catherine muttered miserably, and he laughed again, this time with almost malicious amusement.

'Back to your own little house or back to Ravenhall? You're not sure which is home now, are you?'

CHAPTER EIGHT

CATHERINE was trying to think of an answer when a rather noisy group came in, and it was impossible to mistake Leonie Saddler right in the middle of them. Disappointment washed over Catherine. She had been fooling herself that he had brought her here because it was a special place. Obviously he came here with Leonie too; at least, she seemed quite at home at once. She saw them too, and nothing would have stopped her coming right across.

'Darling! You brought out your little secretary!'

It was said so loudly that Catherine's cheeks flushed hotly. Leonie was laughing as if it were a huge joke, and it made Catherine feel out of place, like Cinderella. She felt that every eye was turned on her, and Damon stopped dancing as he answered Leonie.

'We're taking a night off. Mrs Jarvis is having a rest.'

'Why don't you join us?' Leonie asked, turning her spiteful blue eyes on Catherine, but Damon refused.

'Thank you, but we're just about to go. In any case, I see you're with your blue-blooded friends. You know I don't care for that crowd.'

'I'm only with Colin,' Leonie said with a pouting look. 'I would have been with you if you'd rung earlier. There's nothing to stop you joining us, though.'

There was a satisfied look about her that told Catherine she was dangling Damon at the end of a string. She also knew now that he had asked her out because Leonie already had a date. She felt nothing but misery then, and she tried to move away, but his hand tightened on her arm, holding her still.

'Some other time,' he said smoothly, smiling at Leonie. 'Catherine and I are going home.'

Leonie smiled up at him and reached to kiss his cheek.

'I'll ring you tomorrow,' she promised in a low voice. It excluded Catherine completely and, as Damon's hand left her arm, she turned back to the table. She already knew he moved in a different world from her. None of this should have been a surprise.

So much for a wonderful evening, Catherine mused as they drove back to Ravenhall. Damon had not looked pleased that Leonie was with another man. Maybe he had known she was going to be there. If he had, it just proved how cruel he could be and how he used people, and she had been right there to be used.

It was very dark now, the moon hidden by black clouds. From being a wonderful afternoon and a balmy evening, it now looked as if there would be a storm. It was a fitting end to the day, and Catherine sat silently, trying to fight bitter, restless feelings. There was no future in staying at Ravenhall, because sooner or later Damon would get rid of her, and there would be no job to go back to with the King Group as her post had been filled. He was just keeping her hanging on with some ulterior motive in mind, and she wasn't sure if she could stand it.

As they drew up at the door she turned to him urgently.

'Why are you keeping me at Ravenhall when you have another assistant?' she asked. 'I want to know.'

'We've been through this not very long ago,' he reminded her shortly, but she refused to let it go.

'Not to my satisfaction. Telling me that you've got a plan just won't do. What happens when you've sorted your plan out? My job at the office is taken already. If I'm to get another one I should start looking now.'

There was a brilliant flare of lightning that made her jump, and almost immediately a wild crack of thunder. It was perhaps not the best time to hold a discussion, as she was scared of storms, but she had to know. Damon didn't seem to hear the thunder. His face was thunderous enough.

'I need you here!' She could see his face in the lights from the house, and he was annoyed. 'I'm not ready to let you go.'

'You can't *let* me go,' Catherine told him angrily, annoyed herself at his mean trick in taking her out this evening. 'I work for you. You don't own me. I can leave whenever I wish.'

Damon sat back and looked at her with narrowed eyes, quite clearly deciding to control his temper.

'Tell me why you're suddenly desperate to leave. If Leonie got under your delicate skin——'

'She didn't! What Miss Saddler thinks and does is no concern of mine, as I've told you before. I just work here. I want to know exactly what I'm doing here. I've waited long enough to know.'

'I have no intention of telling you.' The flat way he said it stunned Catherine. There was no sort of compromise. Of course, she could just walk off, but he could make it very difficult for Robin even now.

'*Why*?' She looked at him in astonishment, but he turned away, his jaw tight.

'Maybe I like to see you around the house,' he rasped.

'Like an ornament? Oh, please don't underestimate my intelligence! You had a plan to start with and, knowing you, I expect the plan is still there. Am I supposed to stay quiet and wait like some servant, or should I be grateful for what you've done for Robin and stay grateful for as long as you think fit?'

'I'm perfectly well aware of your thoughts,' he assured her grimly, shooting a furious glance at her. 'I

know you think I'm the worst kind of villain. Well, go
on thinking it, but you stay. I haven't finished with you
by any means.'

She never really had the time to digest that, because
at that moment there was the most horrendous crack of
thunder that came simultaneously with the white flash
of lightning. It seemed to tear across the garden, lighting
up the interior of the car, and Catherine just threw herself
at Damon, tightening her arms around his neck and
burying her face against him.

'Oh, help!' she said wildly, and his arms closed around
her at once as he lifted her closer. From tight anger, he
was now laughing; she could feel it, but she didn't care
at all. She was safe, so long as the lightning didn't get
into the car.

'Can it get in?' she mumbled anxiously, not letting
him go for a minute, too scared to lift her head. 'Is it
true that we're insulated because of the tyres?'

'I've never had the chance to find out.' He said the
words right against her ear, and Catherine started to
shiver, partly from fright, but mostly because his warm
breath against her neck seemed to send waves of feeling
all over her. The rain started in torrents, and she risked
a quick peep out, diving back to the security of his chest
as another flash of lightning gashed the sky.

'I can see us being here all night,' Damon murmured
ironically, but at that moment Catherine didn't care if
they were.

'It doesn't matter. I feel safe.'

'Do you?' He tilted her face up, and she realised then
just how close he was, how near his lips were. 'You feel
safe in the arms of a villain?'

'I—I'm scared of storms...'

'And scared of me,' he concluded, but she shook her
head and went on looking at him.

'No. I'm not scared of you. I used to be, but I'm not now. Sometimes, though, you hurt me.'

'You fight back.'

'I don't really want to,' she whispered. It was like being in a dream where she was able to say anything, because the whole world was in the darkened car with the storm raging around them. Damon went on looking at her for a minute before his dark head bent to hers as he searched for her lips.

She had been hurt, angry and then scared, and she certainly hadn't intended this to happen. It meant nothing, and she knew it, but all the same the wonderful feeling came back, the excitement, the danger and time standing still.

She realised he was being gentle, his lips now brushing her neck, her ears, probing the corners of her eyes, and she let her head fall back, giving in with a little moan that had him tightening her closer.

'I'm dangerous, Catherine,' he murmured against her skin. His hands were holding her head to his, his fingers probing the hollows behind her ears, and Catherine's arms wound again around his neck.

'I know. But this isn't real.' She sighed. 'It's nothing more than a dream. When I wake up it will be all gone.'

'It's real,' he said harshly, 'too damned real! When you wake up it might be too late.' His arms slid around her, tightening her against him as he moved her until she was lying across his body. 'What makes you think I'm immune to silvery eyes and long black hair? How do you know that I'm not keeping you at Ravenhall until I'm ready to seduce you?'

She knew he was trying to shock her, trying to hurt her again, but she looked up at him quietly, her grey eyes shimmering.

'I've never had an affair. It might as well be you. After all, I owe you enough, don't I?'

Damon's hand tightened on her creamy neck, and for a second she thought he was going to kill her. The amber eyes were blazing with anger, but she held them defiantly as she realised that she could hit back too.

It dawned on him just what she was doing, and his tight anger relaxed to watchfulness.

'Don't cross swords with me,' he warned softly, looking into her eyes.

'I'm not scared.'

'You should be. If I take you, I'll keep you. What would you be then, an ornament or a prisoner?'

'I could simply go away,' Catherine whispered, lost in the glow of his eyes and this mad conversation.

'You won't do that, and we both know it. You want to stay.'

His lips came down swiftly to crush her own, and she closed her eyes, giving in to the inevitability of it all. She wanted to be right where she was, and she had probably made that painfully clear for a good while. Right now, though, she didn't even care if he was laughing at her. She didn't care if he despised her. It was a deep hunger that brought an ache to her stomach and a weak feeling to her legs. He was probably pretending to want her, but she wasn't pretending at all.

It was different from the light, searching kisses he had been pressing against her neck, her eyes and ears before. This was Damon as she expected him to be, almost as she had dreamed him. The hard pressure of his mouth was dominant, a drive to impel submission, and when his tongue forced its way between her lips she opened her mouth to enjoy the erotic pleasure of the rhythmic probing.

Her bones seemed to melt and she curled into him, her hand against his face, making an exploration of its own. Her action seemed to take him by surprise, because his body hardened and the pressure of his mouth increased as his fingers slid into her hair, gathering it in his fist, forcing her head even further back.

'Don't encourage me. You should be fighting this,' he growled into her mouth, but she was anxious for more, her face raised eagerly.

'Why?'

'You know damned well why! You know what I want to do to you.' With a groan that seemed to be anger at himself, he captured her mouth again, and this time his hand began to make a slow journey over her body, tracing the contours of her breasts through the thin material of her dress. His thumb found each nipple, teasing it to a high peak as his long fingers cupped and moulded, and Catherine shivered with delight.

Her heart was racing beneath his hand, shafts of pleasure darting through her, making an ache grow between her legs. Her breath was unsteady, a gasp in her throat, and when his hand moved to the rounded swell of her stomach she gave a small cry of pleasure that was almost panic. She had no idea of how to disguise her feelings.

Her hips moved restlessly and his hand slid down her thigh, ruffling the smooth outline of her dress as it moved to his impatient touch. As his fingers encountered the silken skin of her thigh beneath the dress she gasped with shock and then tightened her arms around his neck, so obviously willing that he seemed to come out of some kind of madness.

'No!' He thrust her away from him, sitting her back in her seat, leaning back himself, his breathing erratic. Catherine saw then how taut his expression was, and knew instinctively how much self-control he had exerted to stop. She hadn't even tried to find any control for herself. She had just let the fire catch her.

She sat dazed, looking at him with an innocent wonder that seemed to infuriate him when he turned his eyes in her direction.

'Do you know how close you came to being a victim?' he asked harshly. 'Haven't you any idea at all how to protect yourself?'

'Y-you kissed me,' she whispered. 'It wasn't——'

'Your fault?' he asked savagely. 'You've been giving me longing looks for weeks. I imagine that makes you a typical woman in spite of your appearance.'

Catherine felt shattered. With so few words he made her feel cheap, almost wanton. He had aroused her as she had never been aroused before. It was a feeling completely new to her, and the more devastating because of it. Now he had dashed her to the ground with no mercy.

She gave a choked sob and wrenched open the car door, ignoring the pouring rain, not even noticing the heavy roll of the thunder. It was a few yards to the front door, and before Damon could move she was inside, running across the hall and racing up the stairs. She wanted to hide, never to see him again, never to hear the cruel words said so coldly.

'Catherine!' He called to her as she got to the top of the stairs, but she neither looked around nor paused. There was no way she would ever be able to face him again. She just wanted to hide. Luckily the house was silent. Mrs Jarvis had rooms at the back of the house and might not even be in yet. Catherine felt utterly alone.

In her room she looked around despairingly. There were no locks on these doors. Suppose he came up to continue his cruel taunting? It hadn't exactly been taunting, either. He had left her feeling guilty, as if she had deliberately led him on and then repulsed him. It was the other way around, but she didn't feel up to arguing about it. She fled into the bathroom, snatching up her robe and slamming the door behind her. It had a lock.

It was only then that reaction hit her. Her legs were trembling, she was shaking badly, and she sat on the floor, resting her head against the wall, just letting the tears flow down her face. She had never wanted anyone before in her life, never felt the melting of her limbs, the heat of desire.

He had crushed her so easily and left her helpless. She struggled to her feet, the silent tears still flowing as she undressed, and then stood under the shower. Her mind seemed to be numb. Inexperience made her vulnerable, over-sensitive to harsh words, and she could have expected nothing less from Damon.

His accusation seemed to be hammering through her mind as she dried herself and slipped into her robe. Had she been giving him longing looks, inviting his attention? She just didn't know. She sat on the bathroom stool and sobbed bitterly, even then berating herself. She hadn't cried like this ever, not even when Gramps died. She had always been able to control herself, her fears, her thoughts, her emotions. With Damon she seemed to have no control at all.

She was crying from shame, crying because she felt alone, crying because Damon could so easily dismiss her.

When she finally opened the bathroom door her eyes were red, and her black hair was still wet, hanging down her back and dampening the shoulders of her blue robe. Her lips were pressed tightly together to stem the tears, and she jumped nervously when she saw Damon standing in the middle of her room, watching her.

Escape was her first thought, and she turned frantically back to the only refuge she had been able to find, but before she even got her hand on the bathroom door Damon had grasped her arm and pulled her back towards him.

'Even if you get in there, I'll be here waiting when you come out, however long it takes.' He was being his usual self, dominant, unbending, and Catherine tried to pull away.

'Please!' she begged. 'I don't want to talk to you. I don't want to see you.'

'I can understand that,' he said harshly. 'Just don't look at me, then, but you're not locking yourself back in there. I may be a bloody savage, but I can't stay here listening to you cry your heart out. A few more minutes and I would have smashed the door in.'

Once again it seemed to be her fault. First she was wanton and now she was pitiful.

'I'm sorry for you,' Catherine snapped, still with a sob in her voice. 'The things you have to put up with are incredible!' She wiped the last tears away with the back of her hand, looking utterly vulnerable. 'Just go away and leave me alone.'

He ignored her shaky anger.

'Sometimes a man will do anything to get himself out of a no-win situation,' he said quietly. 'I know I hurt you, but I had to come up for air.' He let her go and turned away. 'You live here, and I owe you some measure of protection, especially from me.'

Catherine turned her back on him, embarrassed and shaken.

'I don't live here. I work here, and please don't bother to pretend. I expect you were right anyway. I don't know how to cope with things like that. Just because I thought you w-wanted me——'

'Thought?' He grasped her shoulder and spun her round, staring at her frustratedly. 'Of course I want you! Do you think I'm superhuman? Don't expect me to give you another demonstration of that particular weakness. Getting out of it once is all I can manage, and you got hurt in the process.'

'I—I don't understand you,' she whispered, and saw impatience slash across his face.

'Don't you?' he asked cynically. His glance slid over her impatiently, and then he turned to the door. 'Maybe you don't, after all. Just go to bed secure in the knowledge that, in spite of your tears, I came out of this in second place.'

'Tomorrow I'd better go home,' Catherine announced shakily. 'It's quite obvious that it would be for the best.'

'I entirely agree. Unfortunately, it would not be best for me. You stay!' He walked out, leaving her shaken and puzzled. She told herself she could just go, but it was not simple at all. Things had become complicated. Her life had entangled itself in Damon's with no hope of her easily getting free, and there was still Robin.

Next morning Catherine made herself go down to breakfast and face Damon, but he wasn't there, and Mrs Jarvis came in to tell her that he had gone to town.

'He says not to expect him back until late,' she told Catherine. 'He'll be out for dinner too.'

Catherine didn't need to be told who he would be dining with, and it merely added to her misery.

By the end of the morning, though, her misery had turned to anger. He was keeping her here for reasons of his own and blaming her for the fact that he had wanted her. She imagined he would want Leonie tonight. When Gordon rang after lunch to ask her out, she agreed very readily. It was an act of defiance, because she knew that Damon would be furious if he knew.

She had no idea why he disliked Gordon, but he did, and there was no mistaking the fact. It gave her a feeling of satisfaction that she could do something he would be annoyed about. It also took away some of the pain when she thought of him with Leonie.

Gordon insisted on picking her up at Ravenhall, and again she did not object, because she now wanted nothing to do with the car that Damon had lent her. She searched out her prettiest dress and spent much longer than usual getting ready, and when Gordon arrived she was waiting. She couldn't deny the feeling of anxiety it gave her to have Gordon once again calling at the house, and she pushed aside the fact that he would also have to bring her back here. She couldn't hurt Damon, but she could annoy him, and it gave her a small amount of satisfaction even though he wasn't there.

They went into London. It was a long time since she had been in the bustle of the city at night, and it was exciting for a while. All the same, she felt very vulnerable, as if she had left part of herself behind, and the small nub of misery grew as she realised she would always feel like this.

Gordon was intent on giving her a good time, however, and she felt the need to make him enjoy the evening even though she wasn't particularly enjoying it herself. After a meal he insisted on taking her to a nightclub, the sort of place she had never visited in her life. The noise was horrendous, especially after the tranquillity of Ravenhall, and she soon became alarmed at the amount Gordon was drinking.

He seemed to expect her to keep up with him too, but she refused as gently as she could, all the time worrying about the return trip. He seemed to be getting more sure of himself, more expansive, as the evening progressed, and by the time they got back to the car Catherine had a pounding headache and felt very nervous.

'How about tomorrow?' Gordon asked as they approached Ravenhall, but Catherine's defiance had melted away as the evening progressed, and she was looking at Gordon with different eyes. He was dangerous in an entirely different way from Damon. There was never any doubt that Damon was always in complete control, but she had grave misgivings about Gordon now. For one thing he had drunk too much, and for another there was a streak in him that she had not noticed before. It was a sort of cold anger.

'I'll be too busy,' she said quickly, and he turned into the drive and stopped the car at once.

'He doesn't keep you working all night, does he?' he asked sarcastically. 'Surely you get time off?'

'Of course I do, but by the evening I'm usually too tired. In any case, sometimes things come up that have to be dealt with. You know what the City is like.'

'I know what Damon King is like, too. There's a lot of speculation about your being here at his house.'

'I don't know what you mean,' Catherine said sharply. 'I'm here as his PA. You know that perfectly well.'

'Do I, gorgeous? What I *do* know is that there's a very efficient lady at the London offices who is also called his PA. I also know that your brother has suddenly become very important in the firm. It's a rare thing to see the boss lowering his dignity to search out a lowly employee. If he wants me, he sends for me, but he goes to look for Robin Farrell and speaks to him very privately. Did you need your brother's approval to live with King?'

'I work for him!' Catherine snapped. 'Now can we get on, please? It's late.'

'Not too late to have a few minutes here,' he muttered, leaning across to her, and as she saw his lips approaching her face Catherine exploded with rage and panic.

In those seconds she knew several things. She knew she could not let anyone kiss her but Damon, she knew that she had completely misjudged Gordon, and she knew she was in a very difficult situation, one she had to escape from rapidly. She ducked out of the way of his searching hands and felt for the door-catch.

'Please, Gordon. I'm very tired,' she said urgently. 'I'll be in trouble if I don't get in soon. You know how awkward Damon can be.'

It was the worst possible thing to say.

'Damon?' He looked at her intently. 'So you're on first name terms with the great King, are you? Maybe I should see what he's getting.'

He made a lunge for her, but Catherine was ready for it. She opened the door and sprang out, snatching her bag and racing off up the drive, praying he would come to his senses and not follow. When she heard the car start she risked a look behind her, but he was reversing to the road, and she slowed down and tried to calm her rapid heartbeats. She felt quite sick, as if she had deliberately invited trouble and had only narrowly escaped.

As the noise of the car sped away, she realised just how long this sweeping drive was, and how late the hour. She was already nervous and shaken, and now the trees she loved so much seemed to be closing in on her; the silence after the car became a menacing silence and not the soothing tranquillity she missed when she was away from Ravenhall.

The sound of her own footsteps on the gravelled drive seemed to be too loud, inviting attention from unknown terrors, and she had to fight hard not to keep up her original mad rush towards the house. She suddenly had the idea that Gordon had simply driven away for a few yards and then come back on foot, and with that thought came the horror of pursuit.

As the lights of the house came into view she began to run madly, falling on the gravel, getting up and running again, and by the time she reached the steps she was shaking and terrified.

Catherine was inside the hall and leaning exhausted against the closed door before she felt at all safe, and she knew that if anything else happened she would just scream. She made her way slowly across to the stairs, but they seemed to be miles away, and she hadn't even got halfway there when the study door opened and Damon stood looking at her in the subdued light, his face less than amused.

'I take it you've been dancing the night away?' he growled, his eyes intent on her.

'Yes. It—it was very nice...' It was all she could do to answer, and his face darkened at the sound of her voice.

'What's wrong with you?' He switched on the main lights, and Catherine winced at the sudden harsh glare on her eyes. It made her want to hide, although she had no idea how she really looked. 'My God!' Damon strode across the hall towards her, and she had the inclination to start running again. 'What happened to you?'

'We had a meal and then—and then went to a nightclub.'

'Stop it, Catherine!' he said furiously. 'Don't imagine for one moment that you're going anywhere without telling me the truth. You look as if you've been in a fight... or were you fighting to get free?' he finished savagely.

'Please don't shout. I—I've got a headache,' she managed shakily, and he switched off the lights, leaving her in the blessedly softer lamplight. It was her chance to escape, and she turned to the stairs, moving as quickly as she could.

'Goodnight.' She was almost whispering, because she was at last on the verge of tears, but Damon didn't even answer, and she knew he was too angry to risk speaking at all. He had a very good idea where she had been and who she had been with. She couldn't expect him to be pleased. He had said she had been giving him looks. Did he now think she had been giving similar looks to Gordon?

When she got to her room she just threw her bag on the bed, and as she caught sight of herself in the mirror she knew exactly why he had been so furious. She looked dreadful. Her hair was all awry around a perfectly white face. There was dirt on one of her cheeks where she had touched it after her fall, and her dress was ruined. The gravel had torn it open in a wide square that would never mend.

It was only then that she realised how much her knee hurt, and she sat on the bed to investigate. It was bleeding, and bits of gravel were embedded into the skin. She touched it and gave a shuddering little cry.

'Leave it!' Damon ordered, walking in with a first-aid box in his hand. She twitched her dress down quickly, and he slanted her a sardonic look. 'You can leave that too. I'm just about to deal with you.'

'I can see to myself,' Catherine protested, but he was already coming back from her bathroom in a very purposeful manner that left no room for thought of defiance.

'Not while I'm here,' he pointed out coldly. 'You'd never be prepared to hurt yourself as much as I'm going to hurt you getting that knee cleaned up.'

He took her wrist and pulled her to her feet, and when she protested further he simply scooped her up into his arms and strode off to the bathroom with her as if she were a doll.

'I'm very strong, Catherine, and very determined. Just give in now and save yourself a lot of trouble.'

Damon stood her by the wash-basin and ran an experienced eye over her, looking for further damage. Then he turned her round away from him.

'Right. Tell your tale and I'll decide what to do about it,' he growled, and she could hear that he was still very angry. Even so, when he slid down the zip of her dress she yelped in a panic. It was too late, though; the dress slipped to the floor, and she was standing in her white lacy slip as he turned her back.

'Sit on the stool and we'll get started,' he ordered icily, and there was nothing for it but to obey. She could have shouted and ordered him out, but she was too shaken for any sort of argument, and the chances of his obeying her were nil. In any case, her legs just folded under her and she was glad to collapse on to the stool.

'You went out with Turner,' he announced, not questioning at all, and she nodded without speaking. Damon looked up at her as he bathed her leg. His face was grim, and she had the feeling that it was only her injury that made him keep his temper under any sort of control. 'And?' he queried.

'Things sort of changed,' she said vaguely. 'At first he was very nice, and then he—he started to drink. He complained that I wasn't talking enough.'

'You were sitting in silence?' Damon asked drily, and she shook her head.

'I thought I was being quite entertaining.'

'Oh, you're very entertaining, Catherine,' Damon agreed bitingly. 'Maybe you weren't saying the things he wanted to hear, however. So he started to drink,' he went on. 'Then what happened?'

'When—when we got to the drive he stopped the car. He wanted me to promise to go out again tomorrow, but I said I would be busy.'

'Why?' Damon snapped out, looking up at her, and she blushed, avoiding his eyes.

'I didn't want to go. He was different. He wasn't at all as I thought. I was a bit scared.'

'So he scared you even more?' Damon asked tightly, and she looked down at her clenched hands.

'I suppose I scared myself. I had to get out fast, and then he drove off and I had to come up the drive in the dark. It seemed a long way, and—and . . . well, I have a good imagination. Just before I got to the house, I fell down.'

She winced as he probed at the gravel, and he was instantly more gentle.

'It's got to be cleaned,' he asserted, and she just bit her lips and stuck it out.

'You're a nuisance, Catherine Farrell,' he announced quietly after a minute. 'You've just about wrecked my plans. I had several things lined up for Turner, and now it seems that a black eye will have to come first.'

'He didn't actually do anything,' Catherine protested worriedly, hearing the grim tone of Damon's voice, and he snapped her a look of extreme irritability.

'Merely because you were quick off the mark, I suspect. I also do not consider leaving a woman out alone in the dark in a lonely place to be a sign of manhood.'

He stood and pulled her to her feet, and Catherine was straight back to embarrassment, looking round frantically for her robe. Damon just stood there, and when she turned he was watching her with half-closed eyes.

'I haven't actually seen you like this before,' he reminded her softly, 'but I've got a vivid imagination too. With you it often goes into overdrive.' Before she could protest he picked her up and walked back into the bedroom. 'I guarantee your safety,' he muttered. 'One attack per night is enough for anyone.'

At the side of the bed he stopped and looked down at her steadily, still holding her in his arms.

'Why did you go out with Turner?' he asked quietly. She remembered then exactly why, and she tried to get away. He merely tightened her to him and went on looking at her. 'Why, Catherine?'

'*You* were out!' The pained words just burst out, and she saw the twisted smile he sometimes had.

'So you were paying me back? Before we know it you'll be ringing round every board meeting, checking that I'm there. Remind me to keep out of mischief in future.'

She just gazed up at him, and he suddenly bent his head and kissed the soft hollow of her neck, his lips lingering sensuously, and she was so attuned to him, so filled with longing, that her reaction was automatic. She gasped, curling against him, her arms coming round his neck because it was as natural as breathing.

'My little innocent,' Damon murmured against her skin. 'It's time somebody took care of you.' He put her into bed and went out, switching off the light and closing the door, and Catherine didn't bother to get up to put her nightie on. It would have been too much trouble. One touch from Damon left her dreamy.

'It's because I love him,' she whispered into the darkness. It seemed completely right. The whole fear of the evening had been wiped out by that one small kiss, as if he knew exactly what to do to make things better.

She tried to feel guilty about Gordon, but after a minute she left the whole idea alone. He had behaved badly, and this time she was not going to blame herself. She thought of the things he had said during the evening, the things he had asked her, but her mind just kept spinning back to Damon until she fell asleep.

CHAPTER NINE

BY NEXT morning, Catherine's leg was sore but not too bad. She was feeling better for a good sleep, and she slid out of bed and put her dressing-gown on, walking to the window to see the garden after the night's storm. Everything seemed greener, brighter. She knew now where every plant was, every bush. It was like her own place, a place she loved, but she knew she would have to go, whatever Damon said.

She couldn't go on staying here when she knew how she felt about him. Things would only get worse, and he was so far from her world that there was no possibility of any happiness, even if he cared about her, which he did not.

At that moment he just opened her door and walked in, and after one startled moment she bridled. Irritation was a good way to protect herself, and she was quite used by now to doing that.

'It's easy enough to knock on a door,' she snapped. It was difficult to stay on an even keel with two amber eyes raking over her, but she managed it.

'It never occurred to me. I usually do what comes naturally. It came naturally just to walk in. Get dressed and come down for breakfast; we're going out.'

Catherine pushed her hands in her pockets and looked straight back at him. He was making her heart race, making her skin tingle, and she just wanted to smile and agree, but she had to leave here. Even at the office they were talking about this arrangement, and she had the

very sound notion that Gordon would fuel any speculation readily now.

'Out is finished,' she informed him seriously. 'The new
expression is "leaving". I've mentioned it several times,
but obviously you keep letting it slip your mind.'

'It was never in my mind,' he said drily. 'You thought
it all up yourself. Keep thinking if it entertains you, but
leave me out of it. I didn't come up for an argument.'

'There is no argument,' Catherine informed him. 'I
simply intend to leave like any other dissatisfied employee. When I come down, I'll type out my notice.'

He took a step towards her, his lips quirking as she
retreated fast.

'I warned you not to cross swords with me,' he reminded her softly. 'Get ready to go out. It's an order.'

'From now on I won't be taking orders,' she told him
firmly. 'I have to leave and I'm going to leave. If you're
thinking it's because of—of last night and the
night——'

Damon pounced on her when she least expected it,
and before she could move he had grasped her waist and
pulled her against him, his eyes gleaming down at her
like gold.

'I *do* think it's because of last night and the one before
that. Don't let it worry you. I can practically guarantee
that it won't happen again.'

Catherine struggled, but it only had him tightening
his grip on her waist. She looked up at him with angry
grey eyes.

'Practically guaranteeing something is not good
enough,' she said crossly, her annoyance growing when
he gave one of his sardonic grins.

'I'm trying not to lie,' he taunted. 'How do I know
what will happen?'

'This isn't funny!' Catherine glared at him. He was
working her up deliberately. 'You don't have to keep

proving that you're despicable; it's understood. I told
you I was leaving, and I've not changed my mind. Now
will you kindly let me go?'

'If you become obedient. Get ready. I'm taking you
out.'

'The last time you took me out it was to further your
own interests. Miss Saddler knew it quite well. You did
it to reprimand her,' Catherine snapped, flushing as she
realised how jealous it sounded.

'I usually do things to further my own interests,' he
agreed, smiling down at her derisively. 'Call her Leonie,
do. It's more friendly. She's sure to like it.'

'I'm leaving today!' Catherine choked, hurt swiftly
by his mocking tone. She struggled to free herself, but
he tightened his grip.

'Of course you're not. You live here. Everybody in
the King Group knows that. I imagined you knew it too.'

Mrs Jarvis walked in at that moment and went very
red as she saw them so close together.

'I'm sorry,' she said breathlessly. 'Mr King said you
had an accident, and your dress——'

'You can throw it out, Mrs Jarvis,' Damon ordered,
letting Catherine go and turning slowly. 'It's ruined.'

Mrs Jarvis just darted into the room and picked up
the dress. She was out without another word, and
Catherine turned on Damon with pink cheeks.

'What will she think?' she asked angrily. 'And you
have no right to dispose of my dress.'

He winced mockingly and then grinned at her.

'Oh, Catherine, the things you say! As to the dress,
do you really want to be reminded about your fright last
night?'

'No.' As usual she gave in, and he went to the door.

'Then where is all this arguing coming from? Just
get ready.'

He had the door closed before she could make any retort, and she suddenly found herself smiling. He could tie her into knots so easily, but she felt closer to Damon than she had felt to anyone in her life.

He always won. Trying to think like Damon was impossible. He was too clever. He was capable of several thoughts to every one of hers, light-years away from her, and she had better remember that, but sometimes she felt as if she was a permanent part of his life.

'Where are we going?' Catherine asked as Damon drove along in silence.

'South. Not too far. There's somebody I want you to meet.' It worried her at once, and she turned sideways to look at him.

'Why?'

'I'm not quite sure,' he said softly. 'Maybe I want to satisfy your curiosity. You seem to think I came from nowhere, appearing one dark night in a black cloak.' It made Catherine laugh in spite of her anxiety, and he shot her a searching look, his eyes lancing over her laughing face. 'I'm taking you to see where my life actually started.'

'We're going to where you were born?' It was some sort of honour; she felt that instinctively. They were not going out on business. As he had said, they were simply going out. Damon was letting his incredible guard down, and she didn't know why.

'No. I wasn't born there. My life started there,' he said grimly. His guard came back up rapidly, and it was the end of the conversation. Catherine stole a glance at him, but he was back to looking like stone. Once again she had managed to say the wrong thing, and it was so exasperating. How would she ever know what to say?

'I seem to have offended once again,' she muttered. 'It's impossible to get close to someone with no clues at all.'

'You want to get close to me, Catherine?' His voice seemed very dark, and she shivered in the sunlight.

'I—I didn't mean...'

He pulled into the side of the road and sat looking at her.

'You did, and it's my turn to ask why.'

'Well, I—I've known you for a good while now and... and I still don't really know you at all. Isn't it normal to want to get to know somebody when you're seeing them every day and—and working for them?'

'You're hedging,' he pointed out drily. 'We were talking about getting close.'

'Isn't it the same thing?' Catherine asked shakily, and he gave one of his low laughs before driving back into the traffic.

'It depends what you mean by "close". We'll continue this interesting conversation at some time in the future, although I must try to remember that you're leaving.'

'I am,' Catherine retorted, blushing when he taunted,

'I'm not ready to let you leave. Mention it again next year.'

They were driving down a street lined with terraces of Victorian houses, not big ones, but the sort that were three storeys high with little gardens at the front and bay windows that looked with secret eyes at the passing traffic. It was a similar neighbourhood to her own, quiet and respectable, but not the sort of place she could imagine Damon visiting.

It was the place, though, as she realised when he stopped the car at the end of a terrace and got out to open the door for her.

'We've arrived,' he pointed out quietly. 'This is where my life began. If you're very good, I'll show you the black cloak.'

They hadn't done more than open the small front gate when the door opened and a woman stood there smiling at them.

'Damon! Back again? I just happened to look out of the front window. Another minute and I would have been round the back and not heard the bell.'

'I can still find the back gate. ' Damon smiled. 'I brought a visitor. This is Catherine.' He looked at Catherine seriously and added, 'Olive is my foster-mother. She brought me up.'

It just stunned Catherine. Thoughts started cart-wheeling through her brain, and she was standing there dazed as her hand was shaken vigorously.

'Damon told me all about you. You're so beautiful, dear.'

'Not too much praise,' Damon ordered. 'She quickly gets out of hand. We came for lunch. What's to eat?'

'He's been saying that for as long as I can remember.' Olive laughed. 'Come through to the back. I'm just setting up the lunch outside. It's a shame to miss this weather. It's cold ham and a mixed salad,' she added for Damon's benefit. 'I made a lemon pie if you fancy that?'

'Of course I fancy that!' Damon glanced at Catherine as he led her indoors. 'Olive's mixed salads contain just about everything. They defy description.'

He was completely at home, more relaxed than Catherine had ever seen, and she knew with no doubt at all that he had thought long and hard before bringing her here. It was his haven, special to him, and she knew he was watching her for reactions.

Olive Milford was just an ordinary woman, in her sixties as far as Catherine could tell. At one time she had been blonde, and there were still traces of gold in her thick white hair. She bustled along in front, chattering away happily, leading them through to the back of the house and out into a long, narrow garden.

'Where's Clive?' Damon asked. He pulled out a chair at the white patio table for Catherine and then perched at the edge of the wall himself. It was a pretty garden, a long, narrow stretch of lawn leading down to a high gate, brilliant flowers on either side and a little stone patio close to the house where they were obviously going to eat lunch.

'Gone to help a neighbour. He'll be back soon,' Olive said briskly.

She went into the house to bring the lunch things, and Damon started wandering round the garden, taking a few dead heads off flowers. Catherine was almost holding her breath. One wrong word and she would destroy all this. She just felt it was for her, special.

Damon glanced at her from under his brows, reading her expression, his eyes holding her wide grey gaze.

'Surprised?' he asked softly.

'Of course. I—I don't know what to say except thank you for bringing me.'

'They won't move from here,' Damon told her, ignoring her thanks and looking up at the house, his eyes going from window to window. 'I've tried to buy them about a hundred other places, and they've viewed them politely but insisted on staying right here. I can understand why. They've never lived anywhere else. Their friends are here. I suppose they have a good deal of sense. In any case, if they moved, a bit of my life would disappear. That was my room.' He pointed, showing her a window at the top of the house. 'From there you can see about a thousand other houses and possibly ten trees.'

'You were happy here?' Catherine asked carefully, but he just shrugged and looked away.

'Eventually. Olive and Clive are very patient people; they needed to be.'

It was too risky to continue the conversation, and Catherine sprang up, making a great show of inspecting the garden. It passed the time until Olive came out with a white cloth and cutlery. With her came a man, and he greeted Damon in the same easy manner.

'Here again?' he taunted. 'I expect the City's shut down.' He was introduced to Catherine, and then turned back to Damon. 'I got the new saw. Come and have a look.'

'Men!' Olive said as they went off and Catherine volunteered to help carry out the lunch things. 'Clive has a workroom in the cellar. He used to spend so much time down there with Damon that I wondered if they would both go colourless.'

'It's hard to imagine Damon doing things like that,' Catherine ventured, and Olive shot her a searching look.

'He can do just about anything. He always could. He's pretty close to Clive. He's never brought anyone else here,' she added quietly. 'You must be special. It was a long time before he brought friends when he was little.'

'Did—did he come to you when he was a baby?' She didn't want to risk prying into Damon's life, but she wanted to understand. He was a different person here, softened, vulnerable, and she could well imagine why he hadn't brought Leonie. Leonie was a part of his present life, not his past. She would look askance at this and these people, or she would laugh that cool laugh of hers.

'No. He was twelve. I couldn't have any children of my own and we fostered quite a few, but after Damon we never had anyone else.' She smiled reminiscently. 'He took to Clive straight away. He was suspicious of me for a while, but after that he was like our own. He just stayed.' She picked up the things and nodded at

Catherine. 'Bring out the salad. We'll just finish and then call those two.'

'Did Damon go to school near here?' Catherine persisted. She had imagined private schools, a pampered existence. It was all so different from anything she had thought of.

'Right down this road. It's still there, updated a bit but basically the same. We had no idea how clever he was until they called us to the school. He was in university almost before we knew it. His mind's like lightning.'

'I know.' Catherine sighed, and Olive laughed, patting her on the arm.

'He's not so frightening, though I expect they still jump when he goes into a boardroom.'

Catherine asked nothing more. She sat at the table and thought about Damon as a boy. Twelve years old. Where had he been until then? He was now not so daunting, even though he was still the dark danger she had recognised from the first. Now, though, he had a past, a recognisable background, and there was a vulnerability about him.

They stayed until late afternoon, and Catherine enjoyed herself all the time. Clive Milford was a very amusing man, and it was obvious that he and Damon were close. When they left she had a bunch of flowers carefully picked from the little garden, and a piece of the lemon pie, carefully wrapped in a napkin. It was so unlike anything she had thought of that it was almost a dream.

Damon didn't say anything, and Catherine sat silently too, thinking things out. In actual fact it had done nothing to make her understand him. In many ways she understood him even less, but he had made a gesture in bringing her to see his past.

'I enjoyed myself,' she said quietly, and he nodded, not looking at her.

'I saw that. Olive thinks you're a great beauty. Obviously Clive's taken with you too. He never cuts his flowers.'

'Was there a test?'

'Who knows?' he murmured. 'If there was, you must have passed it.'

She hadn't meant that. She had been trying to find out why he had taken her there, but Damon was too cagey to give anything away. He was always a mystery.

'I never saw the black cloak,' she joked, and he smiled to himself.

'It's in the cellar. Maybe next time.'

It gave her heart a little flip. Would there be a next time and, if so, what did it mean?

As they got to Ravenhall, Damon glanced at his watch and grimaced.

'I must be slipping. I came damned near to forgetting a meeting.' He seemed to ice over at once, and Catherine knew it was an all-important meeting. It was already late afternoon, so this would go on until very late indeed.

'If you've nothing for me to do, I think I'll go back home and take a look at things,' Catherine said as they walked into the hall. It brought an instant black frown.

'Stay here,' he growled.

'I haven't seen Robin for days. You said I could go out with the car. You said——'

'I want to know you're here tonight,' he told her quietly. 'Tomorrow you can go home to see Robin.' He suddenly smiled. 'You want him here to live with us?'

'I just work here.' Catherine blushed furiously, and he tilted her chin, his eyes roaming over her face.

'All right. I won't tease. Just stay in tonight.' His gaze intensified. 'No dates!'

'I wasn't going to——'

He turned away abruptly, not waiting for her to finish.
'I want to be sure. I'll be back late. I'll see you
tomorrow.'

'Have you found out who it is?' she asked, suddenly
knowing why he was so grim after a lovely day. The
meeting would be about the leak of information.

'I'll be certain tonight,' he muttered. 'I have to see
who's in the trap. Isn't that what hunters do?'

'I never called you a hunter,' she reminded him softly.
'It was always your own idea.' She turned away herself,
embarrassed when she realised she was speaking so fam-
iliarly to him, but he grasped her hand and pulled her
back, looking down at her.

'And what do you think I am? I'm still a black cloud
on your horizon? You knew me even before you saw me,
Catherine, didn't you?'

She never had the chance to answer. He just turned
away and walked up the stairs to get ready, and Catherine
stared after him, puzzled by his mood. She had seen him
in many moods, but she had never felt he wanted approval. Tonight he'd almost seemed to beg for it. Maybe
he regretted now showing her his beginnings, his pre-
vious life. He was not someone who would like to feel
vulnerable.

She sighed and went into the drawing-room. He still
didn't trust her. He had deliberately given her information about his past, and she didn't know if it had
been another of his traps. She would protect him with
her life, but obviously he would never know that.

She seemed to have spent a lot of time in the silent house
lately, Catherine mused as she sat watching television
later. Dinner had been over two hours ago, and still
Damon had not returned. Mrs Jarvis had cleared up and
gone to her own quarters, and now, as on many other
nights, she was alone.

She sat with her feet up, leaning back on the long settee and admitting that she was bored with watching the expensive television that stared back at her. She flicked through the channels with the remote control and then stopped as she came to what seemed to be some glittering occasion.

'At the charity dinner a star-studded cabaret performance was given to entertain the wealthy guests,' the commentator's voice was saying. 'With so many of the rich and famous present it could hardly fail to be a success. At any rate, Damon King, who organised the whole affair for one of his hospital charities, seemed well satisfied.'

Catherine sat up slowly as the camera panned in to Damon. There was no mistake. He was there, and not, as she had imagined, at some important board meeting. She had been worrying about him, anxious to know how things had gone. She was sitting here waiting up, hoping he would tell her, and all the time he was at some glamorous dinner. He was with Leonie Saddler too, and they looked so good together, her blonde hair a sharp contrast to his darkness.

There was a lot of applause, people urging them to begin the dancing like royalty, and Leonie was basking in the glory, turning her face up for Damon to kiss. He was smiling down at her, rich, mysterious, enigmatic, a man from another world, and Catherine felt as if her heart was breaking.

Who was she fooling? For one day she had hoped. She had made so much of the fact that he had taken her to his old home, but it was just his past, a past he knew she could understand.

She switched off and sat staring into space, a sort of panic inside growing by the second. There was no escape, no running away from what was in her heart. She could leave, but Damon would always be in her mind. She had known right from the first that he was far from her, and now it had all been hammered in again. He hadn't even told her the truth about tonight.

The sound of a car about twenty minutes later had her quickly wiping the tears from her face. It sounded like the Mercedes, but she knew that was impossible. She knew exactly where Damon was, and there was no way he could have got here by now.

Catherine hadn't even managed to get to the door of the drawing-room before it opened and Damon was standing there, his eyes running over her. She had put on a very dark blue dress for dinner, and with her black hair around her face, her grey eyes still wet with tears, she looked almost tragic.

'Catherine?' Damon stood at the open door, watching her with a baffled expression on his face. 'What's wrong?'

He came further in, walking towards her, but she just stood and stared at him blankly. It must be some sort of hallucination, an illusion, because he could not have managed to get back here so fast. She knew where he was. He was at the dinner, dancing with Leonie!

'Catherine? You've been crying!' He sounded shocked, and as he reached her she turned away, hiding her face.

'I—I had a headache.'

'And you're crying about it? Stop trying to fool me. I know you, Catherine. You cry if you're hurting inside, not for some pain.' He turned her, looking closely at her downcast face. 'Has somebody been here?'

'No. I've been by myself.' There was just a touch of self-pity in her voice which she instantly heard and wished back, but it was too late; Damon had heard it too, and he tilted her face.

'I can't be in two places at once.'

'I didn't mean that. I never wanted you to be here. What you do is none of my business. In any case, I saw you on television at that glamorous charity dinner. Judith Greaves once told me that you did good by stealth, although that wasn't exactly stealth.'

'So you saw it?' he asked quietly, and Catherine nodded, turning her face away from his restraining hand.

'Yes. It looked exciting. Leonie looked very nice.'

She suddenly realised how jealous it sounded, how childish, and she turned and ran from the room, evading his hand as he reached out to stop her. By the time she was securely in her own room the tears were back in her eyes, but it didn't matter. She was away from him, safe from the all-seeing eyes.

He just walked in behind her and closed the door, smiling ruefully at her shocked expression.

'I told you this morning that I do what comes naturally,' he reminded her. His glance skimmed over her, noting the new tears, and he strode across, cupping her face in his hands. 'Oh, Catherine. What am I going to do with you?' he muttered. 'You're just like a girl. No woman's tricks, no veneer of indifference. You just speak from the heart, don't you?'

'How can you say that? You thought I was full of tricks. You thought I was trying to steal information.' She moved impatiently, anxious about him being so close, but he shook his head, smiling down at her, his hands still warmly round her face.

'Never for a minute. You're like a babe. If you did anything wrong, you'd confess worriedly and expect to be punished.'

Amber eyes moved over her and then he pulled her gently into his arms, holding her close and burying his face against her hair.

'You're very special. Be special to me. I miss you whenever you're not there, Cathy,' he said softly.

It was years since anyone had called her that. It belonged to long ago, to the half-remembered sound of her

mother's voice and her father's. It was gentle and sweet
to hear, but she struggled to free herself, staring up at
him when he looked back down at her with something
like pain on his face.

'You can't be here so soon,' she insisted desperately.
'I saw you at that dinner. It was on television, and you
couldn't have made it back here so soon.'

'And you were crying about it.' He let her go and
stepped to the window, looking down into the darkened
garden. 'You were crying because I was with Leonie, but
you won't let me hold you now. You're jealous, Cathy?
I hope so. I want you to be jealous.'

'To hurt me again? Save yourself the trouble. I was
just interested. I told you I had a headache.'

'You switched off before the end,' he concluded, ignoring her excuses. He turned to watch her closely. 'If
you hadn't, you would have been told that it was re-
corded weeks ago. They only showed it because of the
stars in the cabaret. You didn't watch for long either, or
you would have noticed a lot more than Leonie. It was
black tie. You think I've stopped by a hedge to get
changed?'

'But I thought...' It suddenly dawned on her that he
was wearing a grey suit, the one he had left in, and her
cheeks flushed with confusion. She also felt a great surge
of happiness, but she squashed it quickly.

'You thought I'd lied to you. You thought I was at
some dinner when you were here?' he asked huskily.
'Didn't I tell you just now that I miss you?'

Catherine just looked at him, her cheeks flushed and
her eyes wild. She wanted to run to him, but she hadn't
the nerve. She knew deep inside that all she had to do
was take that step. Damon wouldn't take it, not now. If
there was any chance at all for her, then this was it.

'I'm stupid,' she said hazily, looking down at the floor,
trying to gain some courage.

'You're beautiful,' he said huskily. 'I couldn't wait to get back. For once in my life, the hunting wasn't enough. I want you, Cathy. I can't stop wanting you.'

Catherine just stared at him, her shimmering eyes moving over his face, and then she ran to him, joy racing through her as he gathered her close, his arms tightening almost painfully. He bent his dark head, his lips moving softly over her jawline, his hands stroking her back, and Catherine wrapped her arms around his neck with no thought of pretending.

'I probably owe you a beating,' he murmured thickly, 'but not now. Let me love you.'

There was a pleading in his voice, and she responded to it instinctively. She wanted him to love her, because if it wasn't Damon it would never be anyone else. She tightened her arms round him, and it was all the signal he needed. He swept her off her feet and moved to the bed, pausing before he put her down.

'Why me?' he asked huskily.

'There's nobody else,' she whispered. 'There never has been.' Her hand came to his face, her soft palm stroking his skin. 'Maybe I'm in a trap, hunted and caught.'

'You can step free.' His eyes held hers, and Catherine smiled like a siren, her obvious innocence making her grey-eyed gaze more alluring.

'I want to be caught,' she said softly.

His face darkened and he put her on the bed, coming down beside her and turning her into his arms, holding her so close that she felt every superb muscle in his body.

Instantly she melted submissively, still feeling the dream-like atmosphere that had entered the evening the moment she had seen him.

'Is it real?' she breathed, and he cupped her face with one hand, tilting it until she was looking into his eyes.

'It is,' he said urgently. 'Make sure you know it now, because you'll be another person tomorrow.'

'I won't.' She smiled up at him, her hand touching his face again. 'I'm already another person. I don't want to go back to the past.'

'I couldn't let you,' he assured her fiercely. 'I decided a long time ago that you couldn't go back to the past.' His hands speared into her hair, running it through his fingers as he looked deeply into her eyes. 'But I ask myself if I've forced you into this.'

Catherine wasn't listening; she was smiling, lethargic, ready to step into any danger to be close to Damon. She flung her arms wide, moving against him, her black hair brushing his face, and his control fled away as he began to undress her urgently.

'You've been very close to this for a long time,' he murmured as the last of her skimpy garments fell away at the stroking of his hands. 'Sometimes I've wanted to snatch that damned notebook out of your hands and bring you up to bed in the middle of the afternoon.' He pulled his shirt over his head, and she gasped with pleasure as his skin touched hers.

'I'm cold,' she murmured dreamily.

'Not for long.' He bent his head, his tongue stroking her shoulders, and when his lips moved to her breast she gave a small, excited cry that had him tightening her against him. 'It's all right, darling,' he whispered thickly. 'We'll take it slowly. I know how you feel.'

'You don't! How can you?' Her hands moved to his nape, tightening to pull him back to her, and when he gave a soft groan and came she eagerly opened her mouth to the searching possession of his tongue, letting her own tongue play with his by sheer instinct.

'Cathy!' he muttered desperately. 'You're driving any thought of ''slowly'' right out of my mind.' It gave her a feeling of power and joy that she could make Damon tremble. She could feel his body hardening against her own, his heart beating fast and unevenly. His knee began to nudge her legs apart, and she clung to him as hard as she could, murmuring anxiously when he lifted his head.

He pushed her gently away, moving her clinging arms firmly as he undressed, and then he began to trail kisses down the length of her body. She had thought the heat and desire that burned through her were at their height, but now she knew it was not so. He moved his hands to stroke them over her, following the path of his mouth, as she began to toss restlessly beneath him, and when his mouth found the silky triangle of dark hair that covered her most secret place she moved convulsively, crying his name.

'Damon! No!'

'Yes, darling,' he insisted, looking up at her wild, flushed face. 'I want all of you. Relax.'

But she felt on fire, her whole body pulsating with flame. Her fingers moved frantically into his dark hair, and when his mouth came back to hers she lay against him, pliant and eager, moaning into his mouth as his kisses became more fiercely possessive.

'Cathy!' Damon tore his mouth away from hers to rain kisses on her face and neck, his control almost gone as she tossed beneath him, arching to meet his demanding body. 'Cathy, do you really know what you're doing?' he groaned.

There was an urgency about her that drove every last doubt from his mind, and her answer shattered his final restraint, drove every thought of self-control from his mind.

'Yes, I know. I want to be part of you, closer than I've ever been to anyone.' She gave a little sob of anguish. 'I've never felt like this. If you leave me now...'

'I won't. I won't, darling!'

He possessed her hungrily, stifling her cry of shock with hard, possessive lips, and after the first stab of pain a sweet, honeyed wonder filled her, making her move against him with an equal urgency, her hands urging him even closer. He was inside her, warm, strong, his presence filling her whole being.

'I didn't know,' she gasped, and Damon ran his hands over her, bringing fresh shivers to her heated skin, making her breasts surge against him.

'You still don't,' he whispered. 'Soon you'll know, Cathy.'

He moved inside her until she was feverish and helpless, until all she could do was cling to him and place frantic kisses on his face and shoulders. She was lost, out of the world, tossed in a storm of feeling she had never known, a storm that finally erupted into colours and lights, soaring midnight-darkness that was the sound of Damon's voice moaning her name.

When she opened her eyes he was watching her, the amber eyes clear and searching until she smiled and relaxed beneath him. For a few seconds his lips played with hers, and then he moved away, curling his arm round her and pulling her close again. It was only then that she saw the marks of her nails on his shoulders.

'Oh!' She gave a little cry of distress, and he followed her gaze, glancing down at the marks.

'Yes, you little cat,' he murmured huskily. 'I'll certainly remember you tomorrow.' His hand cupped her flushed face. 'Will you remember me?'

'Oh, please don't talk like that!' The glow died from her eyes, and he quickly kissed her anxieties away before pulling her close again, wrapping her in his arms.

'Go to sleep,' he ordered softly. 'It's going to be morning before we know it.'

'If Mrs Jarvis comes in in the morning...'

'She'll turn and go out again,' he finished sleepily. He reached out and flicked off the lamp. 'Go to sleep, Cathy. I'm just not capable of talking to you now. I've had a very bad evening, and I feel as if I've chased right across the world to get to you.'

'Would you?' she asked softly.

'Yes.' He just breathed the word against her face and then he was asleep, his arms locking her to him.

Cathy's eyes were wide open in the darkness, her gaze turning to the window as the moon finally penetrated the blackness. She never tried to move. She would never try to move from Damon ever. She had felt a part of him for a very long time, and she knew why. Love was bigger, more important, than anything in the world. Her only desire was to be with him always.

Did he feel like that? She had no idea. What would he do—send her away? Keep her here and let things drift along? She could never fit into his sophisticated life, match his brilliance. There was Leonie too. In the heat of desire she had forgotten Leonie but the beautiful, sophisticated face came back into her mind now.

She carefully pulled the sheets over them both, and Damon stirred fretfully, reaching for her.

'I won't let you go, Catherine,' he muttered, his voice telling her he was fast asleep, dreaming. He had said that so often that she knew he was thinking in the past, his dreams not of this moment. What would he say tomorrow? She closed her eyes and snuggled against him, and even in his sleep he relaxed. It gave her some hope, and she drifted into sleep herself.

CHAPTER TEN

WHEN Catherine woke up, Damon had gone. It seemed to be late already, and she looked around her room with dazed eyes. None of his clothes were there, and her own clothes were folded neatly on a chair. Only Damon could have done that, and her panic that it had all been a dream faded. She had no idea what was going to happen now, but, whatever happened, she would never regret last night.

There was a deep sense of belonging inside her, as if some powerful being had folded her close. She smiled at the fanciful thought, and she was still smiling when Damon walked in.

For a moment he stood and looked at her as she sat with the sheets up to her chin, her grey eyes on his face, and then his lips tilted in a smile as he closed the door and walked over to her.

'I've got to get to town,' he told her, looking into her upturned face. 'In any case, if I linger here, Mrs Jarvis might just catch me. Finding me here when you were in a respectable dressing-gown was one thing; this would kill her.'

Catherine blushed deeply, and he sat by her, pulling her into his arms, stroking her tousled black hair from her face.

'Don't go shy on me, Catherine,' he said softly. 'You belong to me.' He looked at her intently. 'Any regrets?'

She shook her head and looked away, but he turned her face back with a gentle hand and forced her to meet his eyes.

'Then don't hide from me. I need you, Cathy.'

'As what?' Catherine asked quietly, soothed by the soft way he said her name, and his gaze lanced over her face, noticing the wistful curve of her mouth.

'As my special talisman, my private angel.' He brushed her lips with his and then caught her close, kissing her deeply. 'When I come back, we've got a lot of talking to do,' he breathed into her mouth. 'There are things you need to know.' He let her go and stood up, his normal manner sliding over him like a cloak. 'You can have the day off, but stay here.'

'Where else would I go?' Catherine asked softly as he reached the door, and he looked round at her steadily.

'Nowhere,' he ordered vibrantly. 'I need you, Catherine. I mean it.'

He was gone before she could reply, and what would she have said anyway? She did not know what her future was or even if there was a future at all. There was still this feeling that she was part of a game that was going on far above her head, but for now he needed her, and she could think of no other life but one with Damon.

Even with the day off there was little spare time. The phone rang constantly, messages came through, and things had to be dealt with. She wondered if Damon's life was ever quiet, and it gave her happiness that she was easing some of the strain.

Gordon rang just before lunch, and at the sound of his voice Catherine stiffened, on the defensive immediately.

'Mr King is not available,' she managed tightly, and he gave a very unpleasant laugh.

'Oh, I know that, Miss Farrell. I know precisely where Mr King is. You don't have to pretend with me either. Call him Damon. We all know what's going on down there.'

'What do you want?' Catherine asked sharply. 'If this is simply an abusive call——'

'I'm not being abusive, Catherine,' he stated caustically. 'I just phoned to let you know that you've ruined your reputation for nothing at all. King's plan came unstuck right from the first.'

'I don't know what you're talking about,' Catherine informed him. At the mention of a plan her heart had almost stopped, and a feeling of doom seemed to seep into the quiet of the room where before there had been peace.

'Maybe you don't,' he snarled. 'You're such a damned little innocent. It's easy enough to pull the wool over your eyes, and King's an expert. You were supposed to set me up, gorgeous. I was supposed to trick information from you. He missed out there, though, didn't he? You're even worse than Judith Greaves. Loyal to the last, the captain's flag flying to the end.' He gave that unpleasant laugh again. 'Well, it's the end now. I got my information from elsewhere. King has no need to keep you at Ravenhall any longer. You'll be out before you can get your wits gathered.'

'You're lying!' Catherine snapped, even though her face was pale. 'Damon wanted me here to help him with work. As to anything else, I don't know what you're talking about.'

'I'm talking about the fact that I've just been dismissed,' Gordon grated. 'Selling information to the enemy is the charge. If he could have had me executed he would; make no mistake about that. Obviously he had a back-up plan and I walked right into the trap. As to lying, I never even came near to falling for the other trick. I knew why you were there from the first day. One of the directors is a good friend of mine, and he talks out of turn. There was some astonishment when King took you on, but he let one thing slip that alerted me.

Apparently your lord and master took one look at you and murmured in his cynical way, ''She'll do''. What do you think you would do for, my dear Catherine? You were the Judas goat, the lovely face that would attract me, and you were deemed to be just stupid enough to be flattered by attention and let slip information that would catch me. King never banked on loyalty.'

Catherine couldn't think of anything to say, because many little puzzles now made sense. She could understand why she had this job when it had seemed so unlikely. She could understand why she had been brought here. And it was not, as she had imagined, so that she could be given free rein to trap herself and Robin. It was to trap Gordon.

No wonder Damon had been surprised and annoyed when Robin had behaved so foolishly. He had known who he was after all the time. It had been Gordon, and now he had him. And she had been supposed idiotically to give information that would catch him in the net. A Judas goat! That was all she had ever been to Damon.

Last night had clearly meant nothing to him but the stirrings of desire, and she had stupidly walked into that too. She had always felt so far from his world, and she was. He had brought her to Ravenhall and then appointed the PA he had already picked out. She was, and always had been, expendable, like so many other people, like so many firms and businesses. Damon had eyed her coldly at the interview and had decided that she would do. It explained everything very starkly.

Catherine just put the phone down and walked out of the study. It was the end of Ravenhall, the end of Damon, and at the moment it felt like the end of her life. One thing was certain: she could not stay here now, not even for another minute. She phoned for a taxi in her own office, and she knew she would be ready when it came. She had few things here.

She had never used the car that Damon had let her have, and even that now took on another aspect. She was probably supposed to have used it to go to meet Gordon more often. She could understand Damon's wrath when she had come in all upset after fleeing from Gordon's car. That would perhaps have been when the back-up plan had been set in motion. She had failed Damon all the way along the line, and he had tricked her with no mercy.

When the taxi came she said goodbye to Mrs Jarvis and left. The housekeeper's kindly face was puzzled, but Catherine told her brightly that she would not be needed here now.

'It was only temporary, Mrs Jarvis,' she said, managing to smile. 'Mr King has a very good PA in London.'

'But I thought that you...' Mrs Jarvis went red, and Catherine knew exactly what she thought. It only stiffened her resolve, and she left without looking back at the house that had become home to her.

By the time the taxi dropped her off, the numb disbelief had faded to misery. She felt betrayed and lost, but there was nowhere to run from the pain inside her. She let herself into the house, glad that Robin was still at work, because she could never tell anyone about Damon and what had happened.

It was like going back in time, so very far back. In the silent house Catherine stood listening, looking around. The feeling was not the same. Her past was all gone. She didn't belong here now. She belonged where Damon was, and that had been a foolish dream, nothing more. There were no ghosts here to cling to, not even the sweet memory of her grandfather. He was now at the back of her mind, gentle and smiling. The face at the front of her mind was dark, handsome, clever and hard.

She didn't even unpack her cases, because everything seemed to be too much trouble. The house wanted cleaning, but she only noted it vaguely, and when she looked through the window the garden stared back at her, a place that needed tending before it became a wilderness.

Perhaps later she would find the energy to get her life together, but right now she could do nothing but stare at the walls, her mind wandering back to the night before and the bliss of Damon's hands on her skin.

It was impossible to cry. Shock had numbed her totally. She made a cup of tea, and even that brought back memories of Damon holding her. Everything about him had been a lie, and she had been too stupid to be even reasonably alert. She had known what he was long before she even saw him, but she had still walked into the trap, and last night she had given her heart away.

Catherine had no idea how long she had been sitting there staring when she heard a key in the lock. It startled her into jumping up, and she was puzzled to find that it was only three o'clock. She dreaded seeing Robin's face as he came in, because it might well be that as he was so early he had been dismissed too. Damon had threatened it long ago, and he never made idle threats.

She was standing like stone, her eyes wide with anxiety, when Damon walked into the room, tossing the keys on to the table.

'Robin's,' he said calmly. 'Remind me to get them back to him or he's not going to be able to get in here tonight.'

'What do you want?' Catherine just stared at him, trying to get her numbed brain working.

'You.' He stood looking at her with that total lack of expression he could call up at will. 'I went home for lunch and discovered that you had only been a temporary help and that your job at Ravenhall was over.' He sat down on the settee, leaned back, and folded his arms behind his head, his eyes never leaving her. 'I then asked myself where an out-of-work PA would go. My next stop was to collect Robin's keys in case you refused to let me in. So here I am; end of story. I came to take you home.'

'What did you tell Robin?' Catherine asked sharply, anger beginning to surface at his calm belief that she would go back. He would change his tune when he realised how much she knew about his black plans.

'I refuse to disclose that information,' Damon stated smoothly. 'It was "men talk", not for innocent ears.'

'Stop treating me like an amiable fool!' Catherine snapped, turning flashing eyes on his unperturbed face. 'I agree that I've behaved like an idiot, but not now. You can go, Mr King! I've resigned.'

'I haven't,' Damon assured her softly. 'I'm your lover and I can't resign. I need the job.'

Catherine's face flooded with colour and she turned away abruptly, no longer able to face the amber eyes.

'Stop pretending,' she choked. 'You tricked me right from the first, and I should have known it. I expected trouble, but I let myself be lulled into—into...'

'Into loving me?' he asked quietly, and Catherine kept her face hidden.

'I don't love you. You're very unlovable.' Anger and hurt gave her the courage to spin round at him. 'Gordon Turner rang me this morning. He told me everything. You took me on for one purpose only—to give information to Gordon idiotically and get him caught!'

'Yes, I did.' He looked at her levelly and the bottom just fell out of her world. Even at this last minute she had been hoping he would deny it, hoping for some other explanation, but he was blandly admitting his cruelty and he didn't even look sorry.

'You're not even going to deny it?' she whispered dully, and he shook his head, watching her all the time.

'I never lie, Catherine. It doesn't seem to me to be worth the trouble. Yes, I took you on to catch Turner. I knew who was leaking information, but he was just too smart to walk into any ordinary trap. He knew better than to try to get round Judith. She was older and very tough. Then you appeared like a gift from the gods. You were beautiful, innocent and totally inexperienced. I knew he would make a play for you, and he did.'

'What a pity you didn't tell me,' Catherine said bitterly, looking away from the cool golden gaze. 'I could have told him just the right things.'

'Not you,' Damon assured her quietly. 'I hadn't known you for more than a few days before I realised my mistake. Catching you was easy, Catherine. I only had to dangle the threat to your brother over your head and you would have walked through fire.'

'And you let me,' Catherine reminded him miserably. 'Why didn't you just get rid of me when you knew I was too stupid to feed information to anyone?'

'Not stupid, Cathy,' he said softly. 'Loyal. Even when you were under threat yourself, you still backed me. As to getting rid of you, I couldn't. Long before you came to Ravenhall, the plan was completely off. I didn't even want to think about you seeing Turner. You were mine.'

'And I walked into that too, didn't I, Mr King?' Catherine blazed. Her innocence now seemed to be almost a crime in her own eyes, and she glared at Damon furiously.

'Call me Damon,' he warned, but she turned away angrily, not even answering.

He reached out with devastating speed and caught her wrist, jerking her off her feet and into his arms as she fell to the settee. 'Call me Damon,' he repeated menacingly, cupping her face in one hard hand and staring down at her flushed face.

'I refuse! You're Mr King, my ex-employer! Why should I call you anything else?'

'Because you love me,' he insisted quietly, his hard hand softening as it slid round her face. 'Because you're mine and I refuse to spend the rest of my life being addressed in such a formal manner.'

'I don't know what you mean...' Catherine began, but he lifted her closer and brushed her face with his lips.

'You do, Cathy. You do,' he said huskily. 'I love you. I need you. If you leave me I'll just follow you, because I'll have nowhere else to go.'

'You'll go to Leonie,' she said unhappily, afraid to believe him. 'You always go to her.'

'I don't.' He smiled down at her gently. 'Mostly I go to Olive. She's known all about Catherine Farrell for a long time. Leonie was the carrot under your nose.'

'Don't you mean the stick to my back?' Catherine asked, finding that she was comfortable and warm in his arms.

'That too.' He laughed. 'I thought you would never love me.'

'But I don't!' Catherine said pertly, deciding it was time that Damon had a few worries.

'Cathy!' he warned quietly, his hand tightening on her face again, and she saw a look at the back of his eyes that melted her heart. It was anxiety. Even the mighty Damon King had worries, and they were about her. 'Tell me!' he demanded, and she smiled into his eyes.

'I told you last night,' she said softly. 'I thought that deeds spoke louder than words.'

'Don't remind me,' he begged urgently. 'I want you now, and that wretched brother of yours will be home soon.' He looked at her with an almost pleading expression. 'I could stand to hear the words.'

'I love you,' she said readily. 'How could I possibly put up with your wicked ways if I didn't?'

'Oh, Cathy!' He rocked her in his arms gently, his face buried in her black hair. 'I'll never let you be hurt again. I'll cherish you all my life.'

'It's a long time,' Catherine reminded him, and he looked down into her face, his eyes holding hers.

'It couldn't possibly be long enough.'

When she was flushed with kisses and Damon let her come up for air, he smiled down at her ruefully.

'I've got to get those keys back to Robin,' he muttered.

'We'll wait for him,' Catherine suggested. 'I can make tea for us.'

'I don't want tea,' Damon assured her. 'I want you, and Robin's not going to be back for a couple of hours yet. I want us to go home.'

It had a wonderful sound, and Catherine stretched contentedly.

'Ring him at the office and tell him we'll leave the keys at the house next door,' she suggested, and Damon moved her firmly from him to stand and go to the phone.

'A brilliant idea produced in the nick of time,' he growled. 'Any more languorous movements and the door would have to be kept locked until morning.'

When they were safely back at Ravenhall, a smiling Mrs Jarvis produced an early dinner, and Damon grinned at Catherine's astonished expression.

'Mrs Jarvis knew you were coming back,' he informed her. 'When she told me her woeful story about your resignation, I assured her that you were just in a bad temper about things. I said you would be back here tonight.'

'How brave of her to produce a dinner on the strength of that,' Catherine said tartly, and his grin widened.

'She knows I always get my own way. She's a romantic soul. Tomorrow she'll be buying a hat for the wedding.'

Catherine dared not speak. It was all too sudden, too much like a dream, and when she looked up Damon's eyes were intently on her face.

He never mentioned it again until they were in his room, the house silent for the night, and then he hovered over her as she gazed up into his face.

'Marry me!' he ordered. 'Marry me soon.'

'Tomorrow if you want,' Catherine said softly, seeing once again the anxiety at the back of his astonishing eyes. 'I'll never leave you in any case. You'd have to send me away.'

'Oh, Cathy, Cathy! I love you, darling,' he confessed huskily. 'I've never put my life into anyone's hands before.'

'It's safe.' She smiled, and his face relaxed as he smiled back.

'I know. But even if it weren't, I couldn't help it.'

'Why me?' Catherine asked, and he laughed, the last sign of strain going.

'Beauty, inside and out. Utter loyalty and a certain something that defies description.'

'Try,' Catherine ordered smugly, and he pulled her into his arms, his wry grin spreading across his face.

'Let's just say that you're sexier in your old dressing-gown than anyone else is in an expensive dinner gown complete with diamonds. Looking back, I suppose I wanted you on sight, but I'm not used to feelings like that. I tend to be on guard. It took me a while to admit how I felt about you, and then I couldn't get you here fast enough. When you told me cheerfully that you'd been out with Turner that time I could have strangled both of you, especially him.'

'I only said it so that you'd think I was capable of going to glamorous places,' Catherine confessed. 'Leonie didn't seem to think I was interesting.'

'Darling,' Damon muttered, 'she doesn't know what interesting is. I didn't even want to let you out of my sight.'

'You didn't much,' Catherine grumbled. 'I assumed it was so that I couldn't get anything for Robin to steal.'

'Don't! It was my insatiable appetite for looking at you. When Turner gave you such a fright I nearly sacked him next day with no evidence at all. Giving him a black eye would have been much more satisfying than dismissing him.'

'We can forget him,' Catherine pronounced firmly, and he held her closely.

'And Leonie,' he assured her. 'From now on there's just the two of us. I only brought her here to make you jealous.'

'You made me miserable,' Catherine complained. 'You made me look a fool in front of her too when you grabbed me and held me in the street.'

'Ah!' Damon looked down at her and smiled ruefully. 'I saw you at the office and I thought you were just a bit too smart for your own good. You had that beautiful hair swept up and you boldly took on the people interviewing you. As you had the nerve to apply for an unadvertised post, I thought you were a bit brash. You fitted the plan perfectly.'

'That doesn't explain your unreasonable attitude to me in the street!' Catherine pointed out.

'It seemed very reasonable to me,' Damon said softly. 'I saw you flying along, your black hair round that beautiful face, and it hit me under the heart. I suddenly knew you were as innocent as a newly opened rose. I wanted to hold you.'

'But you didn't know me!'

'I intended to. That was when I decided to follow my inclinations. Until then, my female companions had been people like Leonie, bored with life and anxious to be rich. And there you were, my sweet, fresh, lovely and oh, so innocent. From that moment there was no plan for you to fit into except being mine.'

'What about Robin?' Catherine wanted to know when she had been thoroughly kissed, and Damon smiled against her skin.

'He'll be very busy. With Turner out of the way there's room for promotion. Robin can move up one notch. It should give him more work and keep him out of our hair. You'll be too busy to mother him, and he'd better get used to hard work. He has to have a suitable status if he wants to be the uncle of my children.'

'You caught him very quickly,' Cathy mused, thinking of Robin's fright and her own.

'Turner,' he said curtly. 'He was the one who caught him, and I wouldn't be surprised if he hadn't been setting your brother up for some time. He knew I was on guard, and Robin was the perfect person to take the blame. Fortunately I wasn't fooled.'

'But who leaked the story about Foster and Brown?' Cathy wanted to know. 'I thought that only you and I knew about it.'

'Oh, I leaked that,' Damon assured her smugly, laughing down at her when she gasped in surprise. 'I leaked it to one person only—one of the directors. He talks too much. I then followed the trail, and it was fascinating. Turner expected to make a killing with that. What happened was that several greedy fingers got burned.'

'You're quite fierce, aren't you?' Catherine exclaimed, looking up at him with a certain amount of awe.

'Hard as nails,' he agreed cheerfully, 'until I see you.'

* * *

Late in the night, as Cathy lay dreamily in Damon's arms, she voiced the thought that had been in her head for some days.

'Why did you only go to Olive and Clive when you were twelve? Tell me about your parents, Damon.'

She expected him to stiffen up, to close her out, but he didn't.

'My parents died, like yours. Unlike you, though, I didn't have a grandfather to care for me. There was no provision for me at all, so I was sent to a home. I was five, and I had memories. I suppose I felt betrayed. I don't know how other children deal with things like that, but I became difficult. I was in several foster homes, but nobody could cope with me. I didn't want them to. As far as I was concerned I was better off alone; you don't get hurt that way.'

'But Clive and Olive coped with you,' Catherine said softly.

'Finally.' He laughed. 'But not before I'd disrupted their lives and caused a lot of problems at school.'

'They love you.'

'It dawned on me slowly,' he confessed. 'Things changed then, but I'm still an awkward customer, Cathy.'

He looked at her with a trace of concern, a query at the back of his eyes, and Catherine's smile winged out to him.

'I've always had this odd urge to protect you,' she revealed. 'Even when you scared me I wanted to protect you.'

'My private angel.' He pulled her close, his lips against her hair. 'Will you go on feeling like that?'

'As long as I love you, which we're both agreed will be forever.'

Damon kissed her deeply and then switched out the light before drawing her back into his arms.

'It's nearly three o'clock,' he muttered. 'We've got to sleep, my love. Tomorrow I have worlds to conquer.'

'You can have tomorrow off,' Catherine said firmly, winding her arms round him. 'We have our own plans to make. I'll cancel your appointments and the City can catch its breath.'

'Yes, Miss Farrell,' Damon murmured, searching for her lips. 'In that case I don't need any sleep. Tomorrow you can deal with everything; right now I'll follow my inclinations.'

Catherine smiled and moved against him willingly. She could sense the peace of Ravenhall around her, and Damon's arms held her fast. Tomorrow they would plan a wonderful new life, but tomorrow was a long way off.

'I love you,' Damon breathed as her lips met his, and she knew it was true. Problems were over. Her fanciful thoughts had been real. A powerful being had folded her close, surrounded her with love, and it would never end.

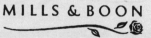

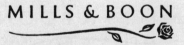

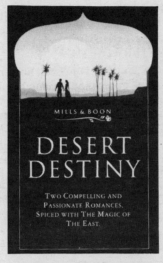
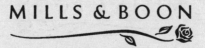

Accept 4 FREE Romances and 2 FREE gifts

FROM READER SERVICE

Here's an irresistible invitation from Mills & Boon. Please accept our offer of 4 FREE Romances, a CUDDLY TEDDY and a special MYSTERY GIFT! Then, if you choose, go on to enjoy 6 captivating Romances every month for just £1.90 each, postage and packing FREE. Plus our FREE Newsletter with author news, competitions and much more.

Send the coupon below to: Mills & Boon Reader Service, FREEPOST, PO Box 236, Croydon, Surrey CR9 9EL.

Yes! Please rush me 4 FREE Romances and 2 FREE gifts! Please also reserve me a Reader Service subscription. If I decide to subscribe I can look forward to receiving 6 brand new Romances for just £11.40 each month, post and packing FREE. If I decide not to subscribe I shall write to you within 10 days - I can keep the free books and gifts whatever I choose. I may cancel or suspend my subscription at any time. I am over 18 years of age.

Ms/Mrs/Miss/Mr _____ EP70R

Address _____

_____

Postcode _____ Signature _____